Quinton

Hathaway House, Book 17

Dale Mayer

QUINTON: HATHAWAY HOUSE, BOOK 17
Beverly Dale Mayer
Valley Publishing Ltd.

ISBN-13: 978-1-773365-81-7
Print Edition

Books in This Series

About This Book

Welcome to Hathaway House. Rehab Center. Safe Haven. Second chance at life and love.

Quinton had been a patient at Hathaway House in its first year. When she finally healed enough to move on with her life, she went into law and plowed forward. However, plowing forward may not have been the best answer for her physical injuries. While visiting Stan at the center, she collapses on her way to her brother's room, as he's a patient here now. The collapse shows a long-term issue, now an acute problem. After talking to Dani and Shane, Quinton's booked back into the center on a short-term basis.

Stan hurts for Quinton. She's an old friend, and he's watched her progress from his first year in business at Hathaway. He'd always had a crush on her but figured his window of opportunity had passed. Now with her once again as a patient, it feels like a second chance for a personal relationship, one he's more than willing to take.

Between her brother—who's not getting along at the center—and Quinton's own struggles to get back on her feet, thankfully she also has Stan and other old friends around, as Quinton takes the steps necessary to put her life back on track … in all ways.

Sign up to be notified of all Dale's releases here!
https://geni.us/DaleNews

QUINTON WALKED THROUGH the front door of the center, stopped, and looked around. When the receptionist looked up at her, Quinton replied, "I'm looking for Stan. And Shane."

"Stan's downstairs. Let me see where Shane is." The receptionist began clicking her keyboard. "He's booked up with rehab patients for the rest of the day. Unless you are one of his patients too?"

"I didn't have an appointment, but I thought I'd ask while I was here. So I'll just speak to Stan today."

The receptionist nodded. "He's downstairs."

"Downstairs?"

"Are you … Did you bring an animal for him?"

"No. I'm a lawyer."

"*Uh-oh.* Is he in trouble?"

Quinton laughed. "Interesting response but, no, he's not in trouble. I am supposed to meet him here today. I am not exactly sure where to find him at this hour but his clinic will be the most likely."

"I just saw him go downstairs," she explained. "I'll let him know you're here."

"Thanks." Smiling, she headed downstairs, looking for Stan. She'd met him a couple times at her office. But this time, with the paperwork, it was easier to just run by, and she was in the neighborhood. This way she could see what kind of operation he was really running and also get his signatures in person. As she walked through the double doors, she found another reception area. Waiting for the woman to get the message to Stan, Quinton wandered around and looked at the place. It was clean. It was efficient. People were standing outside. People were laughing, joking. No surprise there.

A dog was in the waiting room. Poor thing looked like she was terrorized just being here. But the owner was trying to reassure her and to cuddle her and to make her feel better. By the time the connecting door opened, and the woman and her dog were led to another room, Quinton wondered how long she would have to wait. She got up, walked to the receptionist again.

Just then Stan walked out through the connecting door and saw her. "Quinton, how are you?" he asked. "Come on in. I just got your message. I'm sorry if you've been waiting long."

She smiled. "It's all right. I wanted to see the place, what you were running here anyway. I've been here quite a few times but there are always expansions, renovations and improvements to see. It always seems to be so much more than when I was here before."

"It's quite something now, isn't it?" he asked. "Wouldn't have been here without all the donors though. And Dani," he added, with an eye roll. "She's upstairs right now. Do you need to see her?" he asked, twisting to raise his eyebrows.

Quinton shook her head. "Nope, I don't think so, at least not this time."

"Good," he noted. "Pinning her down is almost as bad as pinning me down."

"I'll make note of that," Quinton teased. "This is beautiful here. You've done so much."

"Well, we've still got a ways to go," he added. "And you said you had paperwork for me?"

She nodded, realizing that he probably had a full schedule ahead of him. "Yep, I do." She dug in her briefcase and gave him a folder.

"Okay I can go over these now. You didn't have to come by. You could have just sent them over."

"My brother's up there." She pointed upstairs. "And he's not too happy about it."

"Not too happy to be here or not too happy to be in this situation?"

"Not too happy to be in this situation," she confirmed. "Matter of fact, he's definitely not an easy person to be with."

"Interesting," he murmured. "Well, as you know, he'll get the best care here."

"I also wanted to talk to Shane, if I could get a moment with him, but the receptionist confirmed he's booked all day," she said. "As much as I've had some improvements, I've also had some setbacks, so I need Shane's help. I know he's here a lot."

"Full-time." Stan nodded. "I'm sure he'd want to talk to you. Particularly as you're an old—*previous*—patient."

"I am, indeed, *old* at least." She rolled her eyes.

He burst out laughing. "You don't look a day over thirty."

"Well, it's been many a day over thirty," she admitted, "and nothing like injuries to age you faster than you would like."

"True enough. And stress." He pointed at his head. "I'm

not old myself, but, man, this white hair—which is a family trait—certainly doesn't help it."

"It's distinguished looking," she replied graciously.

He burst out laughing. "Well, that's one nice thing to call it." He grinned. "I knew I liked you."

At that, she smiled, then got back to business. "Paperwork?"

"Absolutely. Come on back to my office. Let's take care of business first." He led her to his office, where they both sat, while he read through the paperwork. Soon he nodded and signed the last page, initialing all the preceding pages. "Thank you, Quinton."

And, with that done, she stood. "Now you can get back to your patients."

"Ah, yes. I've got quite a roster coming up, but I've got a new vet coming along here pretty quickly," he noted. "And I'm looking forward to getting the help."

"Dani's fiancé, right?"

"That's correct," he said, with a smile. Stan escorted her to the elevator. "Let me know when you think you'll be in this area again, and I'll check with Shane about his schedule."

"I hate to even contact him," she noted. "I know how busy this place is."

"Let me talk to him and see when he's got an opening and I'll let you know."

"Thank you," she said. "Much appreciated." She looked around and smiled. "It really is a beautiful job you're doing here."

"It's a necessary one," he replied, "and when you're doing things for the right reasons ..."

She nodded. "I agree with that wholeheartedly. Maybe

I'll go see my brother while I'm here."

"What's his name?"

"Ryatt," she said. "He's only been here a couple weeks. But he's not making life easy for the others. I need to step in and maybe remind him that he doesn't have to be here if he doesn't want to and that he's taking a spot from somebody who could use it."

"Ouch, that would be some tough love," Stan noted, "because really this is the best place for him to be."

"I know it," she stated, "and I'm the one who convinced him to try to get in. Makes me sad to know he's wasting the opportunity he has here." She sighed and shook her head. "But, hey, that's not today's issue. I'll just stop in and say hey."

"I'll call you as soon as I talk to Shane," he promised. And, with that, he watched as she left.

QUINTON WAS A fine-looking woman. Even more, she and Stan had clicked right from the beginning. He'd kind of hoped that maybe he could persuade her to go out with him once or twice. But to have her come here, where he worked, whether to visit her brother or to stay as a returning patient, that'd be perfect. She'd get the best help possible, while Stan had guaranteed time to see her.

He rubbed his hands together. Maybe things would turn in his direction for once.

Chapter 1

QUINTON METZNER HEADED outside to enjoy the fresh air and the beautiful surroundings, as she went to Dani's office. Every time Quinton came to see her brother, Ryatt, she also stopped in to visit with Dani, if possible. It was nice to see the others from back then too, like Stan, even though it was a time of harsh physical healing, which was behind her now. Quinton had been one of the first patients at Hathaway some eight or so years ago. It had grown so much and done so well since then that it continuously amazed her. As she walked up the ramp to the front entrance and the office area, she felt her back and knee twinging again.

Her VA doctor had told her that he could do nothing more for her, and she'd gone to chiropractors and done physio in the intervening years for tune-ups, but her hip, shoulder, and spine were getting much worse. And this worried her greatly. First, she thought that her rehab and her prosthetic had taken care of all those issues years ago. Second, her job didn't understand absences for any reason. Third, she didn't deal well with weakness in anyone, especially herself.

At the main entrance to the center—for the human patients and their visitors—she took several deep breaths to calm her fears and then pulled open the door and stepped inside. The receptionist's desk was empty. She looked around and heard voices coming from Dani's office. She walked over and knocked gently on the door. When it was opened, the receptionist from the front desk stepped out, smiled at her, and ran back to her desk. Quinton glanced in to see Dani sitting there, her face buried in her hands. "Bad timing?" Quinton asked gently.

Dani looked up in surprise, and then her face lit up. "Quinton, how are you?" she asked. "Come on in."

"If you're busy, I can leave," she said. "I came to see Ryatt. I understand he's being difficult."

At that, Dani winced.

"I'm sorry about that. My brother is not doing well mentally or emotionally. I was trying to help him by getting him in here, where I thought he would do so much better."

"And that's our wish," Dani noted. "And there's definitely an adjustment period. Plus some people take longer to acclimate." She motioned at the chair in front of her. "Take a seat if you have time to visit." Quinton stepped forward and then winced again, feeling the shudders ripple up her spine at the moment. "Actually I might be better off if I stop in at my brother's and then head home." She slowly rubbed her hip. "I have to admit that some of my injuries have been acting up quite badly lately."

Dani immediately hopped up. "Hey, are you okay, or do you need help?"

"No, I should be fine." Quinton gave her a reassuring look and a wave of her hand. "I'll just say hi to my brother and then head out." As she spun around, she cried out, the pains shooting up her hip and down again. And, without realizing how, she found herself on the ground, trembling.

Dani raced around her desk, flew to Quinton, and

shouted down the hallway. Before long Quinton was surrounded by people.

Embarrassed, she tried to sit up. "I'm fine, honest," she murmured.

Shane, however, stood at her feet, glaring at her. "You are not fine. Lie down," he barked.

She glared right back at him, but she did lay down again.

"Have you had more trouble?"

She looked over at Dani, wincing and gasping.

Dani turned to Shane and explained, "She was just saying that she's been having quite a bit of trouble with her old injuries," she murmured. "I invited her to sit down for a visit, but it looked like pain was hitting her. So she wanted to say hi to Ryatt and leave afterward. Then she collapsed."

"Well, at the moment, you're not going anywhere," Shane murmured, still staring at Quinton.

"I'm sure I can't stay here," Quinton noted on a hiccoughing laugh. "I was a patient for a very long time. Remember? But I'm not now."

"That doesn't mean we can't get you a room and take a look at what's going on," Dani argued. "And you're still a veteran, and you still get medical, and you still need care. Anybody who thinks otherwise is wrong. Sometimes these issues are lifelong."

"And that's pretty depressing," Quinton murmured. "I wasn't expecting to collapse here. I'm kind of embarrassed."

"Of all the places to fall, this is your best option," Dani stated. "And falling here is the last thing that should be on your mind."

Shane nodded at someone behind Quinton, and a wheelchair was brought around. She immediately protested. Shane placed a hand on her shoulder. "Stop."

She glared at him but subsided again. "I forgot what it was like to feel so helpless," she murmured.

"And maybe you've also forgotten," Shane added, "what it is to accept help."

With his assistance, she was lifted up, until she sagged into the wheelchair. Then she was led to a room right around the corner.

There, Shane helped her get more vertical and out of the wheelchair. But she could hardly even straighten. He immediately scooped her up and laid her down gently on the hospital bed. "Now see if you can find a position that's comfortable."

It took some painful movements and some patience added in place before she managed to straighten out her body enough that she felt no pain. She whispered, "That doesn't feel bad, as long as I don't move."

"And how long has this been going on?" Shane asked, staring at her, studying her body.

"Too long," she admitted. "I did see a VA doctor, and I did see a VA physio, but nothing was really helping."

"And we didn't have an outpatient project back then," he muttered.

"Back then?" she repeated, looking at him in surprise. "Do you now?"

He nodded. "Sometimes people have to return for tune-ups," he stated gently. "Sometimes you forget the lessons that you were taught, and we have to remind you to do them again. Sometimes old injuries like to act up and cause new problems," he explained. "Our outpatient project is still a pilot program, but we've been opening it up more and more."

"So …" And she hesitated. "So now what?"

Just then a shout came from the hallway, and she winced. "That would be Stan, wanting to talk to you."

Shane frowned. "And why is that?"

"He told me that he would mention to you that I'm having some trouble and wondered if there was any way I could have you take a look."

At that, Stan Herzog came in through the door. "I just heard." His gaze went from Quinton to Shane and to Dani, as she left them to handle Quinton. Stan walked to the bed and picked up her hand. "Are you okay?" he murmured gently.

She squeezed his fingers. "Well, outside of being embarrassed, a little bruised, and sore," she shared, "I guess I'm technically back to what I really needed, which was maybe some time with Shane to give me a hand."

Stan immediately looked at Shane and asked, "You can help her, can't you?"

Shane shrugged. "I still don't know what the problem is," he noted, "but we helped her the last time, so, in theory, yes."

"I didn't realize," she whispered to Stan, "that it was possible to get outpatient help here."

Stan turned to Shane. "Is that true?"

Shane shrugged. "We haven't had the program for very long, but it became something that we could see a great need for. So, yes, we're doing it on a temporary basis, while we see how it works and can smooth out some of the wrinkles to provide the best service we can."

"I think obviously it's already something that's needed"—Stan pointed at Quinton—"as you can see."

"I know," Shane confirmed. "And we're seeing more and more of it."

"Is that because the work's not holding?" Stan asked.

Shane shook his head. "No, it isn't. It's just some of these cases are complex. And, when they go to other doctors, they tend to follow what that doctor says, but it's not always what they need. And I'm not bashing the medical profession. Believe me. However, once you've been working with somebody for a long time, you know how their body reacts and how to do a proper tune-up. We should probably start running a few beds on an interim basis just for previous patients we have worked with, whose past symptoms we have knowledge of, and who need to come back after a few years."

"That's not a bad idea," Stan agreed, "because these problems, these injuries, can be all-consuming. So you take them to a certain point and then what?"

Shane turned to Quinton. "Do you have any reason you need to rush home? Like pets to look after or the like?"

She frowned at him. "I wasn't planning on staying the night."

"Maybe you should," Shane stated. "*Do* you have a reason to rush home?"

She sighed and then shook her head. "Tonight, no, not really. But booking myself back in here wasn't exactly something I was planning on. Nor do I have the time for it."

"No, I can see how a surprise hospital stay can interrupt your life and your work," Shane said. "And maybe you wouldn't need to be here for long, but I obviously need some time to figure out what's going on."

"What? You can't wave a magic wand," she replied in a joking manner, "and just tell me exactly what ails me?"

"I can tell you some of it, but I can't tell you all of it. Didn't you have some shards of shrapnel still left inside?"

"Yes." She winced. "The VA doctors all told me that

they couldn't remove it."

"And what if those have moved?"

"Well, I did have X-rays done not too long ago," she shared, "and there didn't appear to be anything like that going on."

"Okay," Shane replied, "but we'll take and examine our own." At the look on her face, he added, "I don't know if you're covered, if that's a financial problem for you, "but it's definitely something I need to see firsthand and a current view."

"Fine," she murmured. "I have insurance. Besides, as Dani just reminded me, I'm a veteran with medical coverage."

"Good enough," Shane replied. "I'll order these now for first thing in the morning."

"Can we do them tonight?" she asked.

"No, sure can't," Shane countered. "The earliest I can get them done is tomorrow morning."

She stared at him and asked, "Can I go home and come back?"

"I don't know," he replied, with a knowing smirk, stepping back and looking at her. "Can you?" And that's where it hung in the air.

Stan looked at her and added, "I know you don't want to stay, but seriously is that what you want to do, to go home only to come back here within hours? Can you drive? I mean, safely?" Stan stared at her but got no response, then turned to Shane.

"I think she can best answer that question."

"Probably not a good idea," she replied. "Yet ..."

"This way you can visit with your brother overnight," Stan suggested.

"That'll make him happy," she murmured in a snide tone.

"You two can have dinner together and get caught up," Stan added.

"I don't know that I can move at all," she finally admitted.

"Well then, guess what?" Stan told her. "I'm bringing dinner here to you tonight."

"Wow. I mean, not to sound ungrateful or anything"—she looked from Stan to Shane and back—"and I really do need the help but …" Then she stopped because it wasn't in her to not show appreciation when they'd gone over and above.

Shane smiled at her. "I get it. You thought you would go home, have a glass of merlot, sit out on the deck, watch the sun come down, maybe have some friends over, do something nice for yourself, have a bath, go to bed, get up, and the grind continues."

"Yeah, something like that." She nodded.

"Well, unfortunately at this point in time," he stated, "you're here right now. And I suggest it'll be … Let's see? Today's Wednesday? So we'll talk about you leaving in time for Monday. That's the *earliest* I see you leaving Hathaway House, and that's *only* after I've seen the X-rays and find that we can get whatever is going on in there straightened out."

She hated to give in, but physically she knew she wouldn't move from this bed tonight—or even beyond. She closed her eyes, whispering, "Could I ask somebody to go to my vehicle and get my purse, my cell phone, and my laptop?"

"I'll go," Stan offered. She gave him her keys, and he disappeared.

Shane looked at her, smiled, and asked, "You and Stan still … friends, *huh?*"

"He's a good man," she replied, feeling heat wash over her face.

"He absolutely is," Shane agreed. "I think he's been carrying a torch for you all this time."

"I don't think so," she retorted, with a laugh. "When I was a patient here, he was busy trying to build up his business downstairs, and I know he was busy, back then and now. It just seemed like we hit it off, and we've been friends ever since. So I try to see him, at least for a moment, every time I come by."

"Yep," Shane agreed. "I have noticed. I've also noticed that he's always happy to see you when you do come by," he added, "and you might want to consider that too." And, with that, he took off.

Quinton was surprised to hear what Shane was implying. It wasn't a bad thing; she always did like Stan. He was a little older than she was, but then she wasn't what she would consider a spring chicken. Her injuries had seriously impeded her progress to move forward in her personal life for a very long time, and, even when she had gotten back on her feet, it's not as if she was immediately young and spry again. It had taken a long time for her to get fully functioning again.

So, with her corporate attorney work, she had seen Stan and Dani over the years. Just not as often. Then Quinton had helped get her brother in here, and that threw her and Stan together again. But maybe it really hadn't. Maybe it was more about coming to see Stan. No, she realized that wasn't true either. But seeing Stan had been a nice side benefit.

When he returned a few minutes later, his arms laden

with her stuff, she grinned. "Thank you so much. I hated to send you out there to run my errands."

He shook his head. "The clinic is closed up," he shared. "We're done for the day anyway. Besides, I would do it for any friend."

At that, her smile dimmed slightly because, of course, he would. He was just that kind of a person, one of those nice people who never seemed to get the appreciation or the understanding that they should. "Well, I do appreciate it. Thanks."

Stan remained in her room, silently considering something. She wondered what.

STAN BELIEVED IN love at first sight. It had happened to him once, long ago. With Quinton. Unfortunately he had never asked her out. He had used one excuse after the other to put it off—because of fear? He sure hoped not. Regardless he had used lame excuses, as he looked back now. He opened his mouth and then closed it quietly, only to begin again. "How about a cup of coffee or something?" he asked gently. "Before the dinner rush starts."

"I won't be going down there," she murmured.

"No, but I'm serious," he stated. "I'm quite happy to bring something back and have dinner with you. I know you'll feel like a fish out of water here at first."

"You're not kidding," she agreed. "I'm still not sure how I managed to be persuaded to stay."

"I think the answer to that's pretty easy," he noted. "Your body betrayed you and was calling out for help."

"Yeah, this broken-down body has suffered more than it

feels like it should."

"You know what? I think bodies are like that. We take care of them to the best of our ability, and, if we do a good job, they can last a long time. However, then life can happen, and sometimes we can't take care of them quite as well as we should."

"I wonder if I did something to bring this on," she murmured.

"Don't even go there," he told her, with a smile. "You've done the best that you can. Now just relax and let Shane and the rest of them figure it out."

She rolled her head to the side.

He'd always admired that classic profile and the silky auburn hair that she kept in a stately bun at the back of her neck. She was the epitome of a lawyer from a distance; he just didn't see how she could do that kind of work. "Honestly," he added. "I mean it. Stop stressing over work. Stop clenching your jaw. Stop feeling guilty. You are in good hands here. Let us help. Including me, just by bringing you dinner to your room for your first night."

"I know that everything you just said is right, and I appreciate all the good thoughts. And I'll take you up on your offer to have dinner with me."

"Good. It's too early yet for the buffet, so, if you need anything now, tell me."

"I wonder if my brother is mobile enough to come down here and visit me instead tonight."

"I don't know," he said. "Shall I go find out?"

She studied him for just a second. "You really don't mind?"

"For you, never," he replied gently. And, with that, he was gone.

She also didn't know for sure if her brother would care enough to see her; he was pissed at her right now, which didn't help. He was a good man but acting out—instead of the responsible young man she knew he could be. When Stan returned a little bit later, she was drowsy, her eyelids already starting to fall shut.

"Are you tired?" he asked. "You want to eat something now instead of later?"

She looked at him. "How late is it?"

"It's just going on five-fifteen now. Dinner buffet will start at seven."

She thought about it and mentioned, "You know what? I don't even think I got lunch." He stopped and looked at her. She shrugged. "It was busy today."

"And you were probably worrying about your brother, weren't you?"

"Well, yes, I was, as soon as I realized he wasn't being a very good patient," she murmured. "I don't know how he gets away with that."

"He does it by not caring about the people around him," Stan stated immediately. "And it's not all that unusual in the initial adjustment period."

"No, but it saddens me. It's a huge opportunity to be here," she murmured. "Did you find him?"

"He was just coming back from a session, and he didn't look all that great," he shared.

"Did you tell him that I'm here?"

"I did. He was stunned for a moment and then said that he'd be down later."

She nodded. "That's good. I would like to see him."

"Is there just the two of you?"

"Yes, now there is, plus an uncle who lives far away. But,

in our immediate family, my parents divorced. My mother took my brother as part of the deal. My father couldn't cope and started drinking heavily, which is one of the reasons that I ended up in the military when I did," she explained. "I was looking for a direction. I was looking for a family."

"And you found it," he reminded her gently. "Don't ever regret what you did."

"No, until I look at my busted-up body and the abuse it took," she noted, with a lopsided smile.

"And sometimes that can happen here anyway. You could have been hit by a car and probably wouldn't have had such a nice spot as Hathaway House to recover in."

"That's true enough," she agreed. Just then they heard a wheelchair.

He looked at her and smiled. "I think that's your brother. Maybe I'll go see how Dennis is doing."

"Find out what's for dinner," she suggested. "I haven't forgotten how good all the meals were."

"When I tell Dennis that you're back, he'll be thrilled." And, with that, Stan disappeared.

<h1 style="text-align:center">Chapter 2</h1>

THE SOUND OF the wheelchair was slow but steady. She listened to it, realizing that it would likely be her brother. When his head poked around the door, he stared at her in astonishment. He rolled closer and whispered, "You okay?"

"I'm okay," she said, feeling fatigue pull at her that she hadn't experienced in a long time.

"What happened?" he asked.

She shrugged and then shuddered with pain, unable to speak.

"Is it the old injuries?"

"I don't know," she murmured. "They'll take X-rays tomorrow."

"Can they? Can you even be here?"

"I don't know. Dani seems to think so. I mean, I spent a lot of time here originally, but the center was nowhere near as big as it is now," she added.

"Is there anything you need?" he asked.

She looked over at him. "Well, it'd be nice if I didn't hear what a mess you were every time I come here, being difficult and all the rest," she murmured. "But, other than that, no. I'll just spend the night, hopefully without a whole lot of pain—although I'm not sure how to make that happen. Then, if I'm lucky, I'll wake up, and everything will be just fine."

"I forget that you spent time here. Like, I know you did, but I wasn't in town at the time, and it just seems odd to see you in a bed as a patient."

"Right? Don't worry. It feels odd for me too."

He frowned again.

"How are you handling life here?" she asked.

"It sucks," he replied bluntly.

"Yes, it does," she murmured, "but you know that you have other alternatives, if you don't want to be here. You don't have to make life miserable for everybody else."

He flushed at that. "I've been to a couple VA centers. Didn't like them much either."

"Nope, nobody does. The issue is more about the fact that you don't like the *position* in life you're in," she explained. "So nothing will be good enough."

"Well, look at you," he pointed out. "How good was it to be here at Hathaway House all those years ago if you're back here again? I mean, obviously it wasn't enough."

"That was more than eight years ago," she argued, her voice stern as she stared down at her kid brother. "My body was younger, in better shape back then. Once I got back to work, it's been go-go-go. I haven't had time to breathe. My body went downhill."

"Yeah, well, maybe it's time you changed jobs."

"Maybe, and do what?" she asked. "I've been doing what I always do, which is the same career I started out in."

"Yeah, but I thought you would do something more aligned with your beliefs, like working on ADA cases or even as an attorney with the ACLU or something. You should enjoy going to work. You wanted to change the world, one downtrodden person at a time. Remember? Not just see it as some time clock and then some race to get out the work as fast and as long as you can. This corporate gig may pay the bills, but the stress is killing you," he stated.

"Maybe, but I don't know what else I'm supposed to do," she murmured. "It's not as if there are a ton of jobs for broken-down vets."

"Don't say that." He winced. "I know because I am in the same boat, and I don't know what I'll do either," he admitted. "I was thinking about an online business."

"And that's possible," she noted, loving that he was at least thinking about his future. "You've always been very good with technology. I don't know if you're still that good within such a competitive field, but I suppose you'd find out pretty fast. Plus you can get further training, using your benefits."

He laughed. "I forgot what a cheerleader you are."

"You mean, like I'm rooting for you until I'm not." She rolled her head to the side and smiled at her brother. "I can be a cheerleader, but I've always been such a realist too, which tends to come through in everything I do."

"Well, the best thing is, if you just don't change," he admitted absentmindedly.

"I need to change apparently," she replied. "Look at me. I'm back in here." And just enough bitterness was in her tone to make her wince too. "Sorry. It's a reality check for me right now. My body is obviously not as strong or as healthy as I had hoped it would be."

"But it's nothing like Mom, right?" he asked hesitantly.

"Breast cancer? I don't think any of this can be attributed to that," she replied, with a wave of her hand. "But, gee, thanks for bringing that thought to the forefront."

He didn't say anything for a long time.

"So what are you going to do?" she asked. "Go or stay?"

He tilted his head. "What do you mean?"

"Well, like I told you, you don't have to stay here at Hathaway House. Yet I can't imagine where else you would go. However, if you're going to stay, you can't make life miserable for everybody. There's too much stress in the world already. We don't get to turn around and make more stress for other people just because we're having a hard time. If you don't want to stay, that's easy enough to fix. Find another VA and transfer," she stated. "Maybe I'll take your bed here." At that, she shifted and then cried out, as the pain washed over her again.

He rolled his wheelchair closer.

She had the one prosthetic still on her right leg. She'd lost it just below the knee. Ryatt had one that he'd lost just above the knee on the left side. His was still a raw stump, whereas hers had healed somewhat, but even now the prosthetic was starting to kill her. "If I could move," she said, "I might take off this leg."

He frowned. "Do you want me to get Shane?"

"No, he's probably having dinner," she replied on a breathy gasp, as she shifted again. She relaxed back and sighed. "Well, maybe I'm sleeping with it on."

"You know that's not going to work," he told her. "I can help get it off."

"No, that's okay," she said. "I'm going to first wait for the pain to ease. Then try."

"Doesn't sound like the pain will go away right now."

"Well, it needs to," she stated, her voice sharp.

He rolled backward. "I'm going to go have dinner. I'll talk to you afterward." And, with that, he disappeared.

She groaned because it seemed like she was always saying

the wrong thing to him at the wrong time. And it was frustrating because he was basically a good guy, and he deserved so much more of her, but today? ... Well, she didn't have much more to give.

When Stan returned, he walked in and then slowed his footsteps. "Are you sleeping?" he asked softly.

"No, I'm not sleeping," she replied. "I was trying to figure out how to get my leg off, so I can sleep for the night. And yet it's still very early, and I shouldn't even be thinking about sleeping yet."

"You're injured," Stan said. "Sleep whenever your body wants it. And I suspect that you've probably been working too many hours and too many nights, trying to do whatever it is that you think you need to do."

"Isn't that what life is?" she asked. "Just a whole series of doing too much?"

"Maybe," he murmured. "Yet I don't think it has to be."

She smiled, as she looked over at him. "Maybe not, but it seems like life is just go-go-go-go."

"That's fine if you're at maximum strength and health," he agreed, "but, when you're not, it becomes an added stress all on its own."

Her gaze shadowed as she considered that, and said, "Well, I hope not."

"Let me go see if I can find Shane." And he didn't give her a chance to argue; he just took off.

She groaned, while admitting she really did need help tonight, as much as she hated it. She was not much better off than when she'd first arrived at Hathaway House so many years ago. That was depressing. She closed her eyes and tried to rest.

STAN RACED TO the physio offices. There he found Shane, doing paperwork.

Shane looked up, frowned, and asked, "Is she okay?"

"She can barely move." His hands were on his hips, as he glowered at Shane. "I don't know if she's just done too much or what, but she can't even begin to take off her prosthetic leg by herself. And she's being so stubborn about refusing to ask for help—or for painkillers. So I'm wondering if you can give her a hand."

Shane stood. "Absolutely, but it's something that anybody can do."

"I'm not so sure about that. She seems to think that it was more help than her brother could give her. And she's the type to help everyone. So, when she needs help, why don't they return the favor?"

"Well, if she's the one usually in the position to assist others, then this reversal of roles could be just something she doesn't want her brother to see—a sign of weakness or whatever," he muttered. The two men walked back into Quinton's room, and her eyelids flew open.

QUINTON TOOK ONE look at Stan and Shane, then frowned. "You know that, if I just lay here quiet for a bit, I could probably get it."

"You *could* probably get it," Shane agreed. "However, if you never ask for help, especially when you need it, then I foresee more than just physical problems here."

That made Quinton immediately gear up the attorney

side of her to argue with that assessment.

Shane raised one finger to shush her, then gently pushed her pant leg over the top of her prosthetic and asked, "Did you hurt this recently?"

She shook her head. "No, I don't think so."

He looked at it closely and raised one eyebrow. "The prosthetic could be part of your main problem."

"Why is that?"

"Because the whole alignment is off," he said, "not in a big way, just enough that your structural alignment would go out the window with it." He quickly pushed the button to release the prosthetic then slowly rolled the sock down off her stump.

She cried out softly with relief. "Ah, that feels better."

He looked at her stump and noted, "You realize you've got a really big blister back here too, don't you?" He lifted the leg up and showed Stan a good two-inch-wide blister.

"It was getting sore, but I don't know about a blister."

"You've got a good one," Stan said, looking at her. "It looks pretty nasty." He took a picture of it on his cell phone and then held it out for her to see.

She stared at it in shock. "Where'd that come from?"

"Are you sure you didn't fall or have in any way damaged the prosthetic that you remember?" Shane asked.

She shook her head. "Not that I remember, no." And then she frowned. "Except I did fall down a couple risers on the stairs."

Both men stared at her in shock.

She shrugged. "I didn't really think anything of it. I mean, obviously it wasn't a great moment. But I was alone, I hopped up, straightened up, and carried on."

"And how long ago was that?"

"It was about …" She stopped, thought about it. "I don't know, maybe four, five months. It wouldn't be from that, would it?"

"It could easily have been that," Shane stated, "particularly when this fall caused a small adjustment to your prosthetic. Then, over time, your body goes out of alignment. That would make it pretty easy to become an even bigger problem."

"Well, in that case then," she replied, "I guess I did this to myself."

Shane stood at the end of her bed, his arms crossed over his chest. "So tell me honestly. What would you say your regular workday is like?"

"What do you mean?" she asked.

"I'm trying to get a picture of a woman, who has a two-inch sore on her leg, who fell down the stairs, who got up, who didn't think anything of it, who slowly put her own alignment out of whack, and who didn't notice the increase in pain *nor* the decrease in movement."

She stared at him, slowly understanding what he was getting at. A flush rose up her neck. "So what do you want me to say? Obviously I'm a person who's not very aware," she muttered.

"But why?" Shane asked gently.

She looked over at Stan, who still stood here beside them. "Probably," she added carefully, "because I'm very busy."

"As in too busy to look after yourself?" Shane asked.

She glared at him. "I think the answer to that is evident," she snapped, mostly mad at herself. "I obviously haven't been doing a good job, if that's what you found. I still don't understand how I could have walked around and not noticed that thing."

"Yeah, me too. I know you have nerve damage on the back, but that's a pretty major blister. And it is fresh," he noted. "So it could have been just even part of today. Still, I've got nurses coming to draw some blood and to give you some muscle relaxants. We're going to run a bunch of tests, take X-rays tomorrow, and just see where you're at. For tonight," he added, "I suggest you eat, relax, and try to sleep if you can. A set of pajamas are in the bathroom for you. I think an extra set of comfy clothes are in the closet too. Call for a nurse to help you."

She nodded slowly but was obviously pretty distressed by the whole thing.

Shane reached down, gently patted her good leg, and smiled. "We'll look at it all tomorrow. It'll be a whole new day. So get some rest, and we'll see how we can fix you up, after we get more info. And, if you need something more, like heavy-duty painkillers, let me know immediately. Don't put that off either."

Stan leaned over, gave her a quick hug. "I'll be back later to see if you are awake enough for dinner." And he walked out behind Shane.

Chapter 3

QUINTON OPENED HER eyes the next morning—still dressed in yesterday's clothes—surprised and gratified that she had slept and pretty decently, all things considered. Of course she hadn't moved yet, and that was a concern because now her bladder was screaming at her. She noted the crutches nearby. Shane must have left them for her last night, after she fell asleep.

Moving as carefully as she could, she shifted in the bed, shocked that there wasn't agonizing pain right off the bat. As she got up, grabbed the crutches, and made her way to the bathroom, her joy turned to concern.

Because, although her level of pain was better, it was a long way away from good.

She made her way back to the bed, sat down on the edge, wondering what she was supposed to do now. She checked her watch, and it was after 7:00 a.m. That should, in theory, mean that she was eligible for breakfast, but she wasn't sure that she was up for the trip or for dealing with the public.

The minute any of the medical personnel came to her room, she imagined there would be a ton of questions, and that wasn't something she particularly wanted to face either. And yet why not? She had been planning on talking to Shane about her problems as it was. But it seemed wrong, it felt wrong, and she just struggled to get over that. And it was making itself more of a problem. She would have to deal with whatever all that was later.

Meanwhile she was willing to do what she had to for a cup of coffee. She made her way to the wheelchair, realizing that no way she could possibly crutch all the way down to the dining area. She didn't want to drink her coffee there. So how would she carry hot coffee back to her room on crutches? Nor was she up for putting the prosthetic back on. And that in itself was sobering. But the coffee still called her.

She slid into the wheelchair, realizing just how natural it still felt. Even after all these years of getting herself back up on her feet and trying hard to have a normal life again, as soon as she sat down in the wheelchair, it was just like old times. That was a sobering reality too. She thought that she'd be well past it. And instead she had never left it at all.

Moving quietly, she rolled out of her room, awkwardly trying to open the door, at the same time realizing that, although it felt like maybe she hadn't left her wheelchair at all, she had fallen behind on the accompanying skills in navigating a wheelchair. So this wouldn't be the simple journey that she had hoped it would be.

She just wanted a cup of coffee, for crying out loud.

Sadly, frustration was something she was long used to.

She made her way out into the hallway and slowly down to the area where she knew the dining room would be.

As she approached, she heard a few voices, but it was pretty quiet, which was good. Maybe she could grab a coffee and get out without seeing anyone. She really didn't want to deal with a crush of people. *Would anybody really recognize me now?* She would just be another face. She knew that, and this wasn't necessarily even a problem to waste her time worrying about. It's just, for her own mental health, she didn't want to appear to be imposing in any way.

As she slowly moved her way into the dining room section, she heard a gasp. She looked up, and there was Dennis. He bolted from around the corner, and, as soon as he got toward her, she opened her arms, feeling tears in the corner of her eyes. There was just something so caring about this man. Not in the same way that Stan cared. Dennis was a friend. She felt infinitely casual around Dennis. But Stan? No. She felt anything but casual around Stan.

Dennis hugged her gently. "Somebody told me that you were back for a tune-up," he said. "I hadn't realized it was this serious."

"And I don't know if it is," she admitted, with a wry smile. "I spent the night because I pretty well collapsed when I went to talk to Dani." She shrugged. "So they gave me a bed for the night, and now I find I'm not really capable of doing too much more."

"You could have called for a coffee, you know?"

"You remember my caffeine addiction, do you?"

He laughed. "Of course," he agreed. "Besides, as you know, nowhere near the same number of people were here back then that are here now," he explained. "We did get to know everybody a little bit more back then."

"Oh, I don't know," she replied, with a gentle smile. "You treat everybody the same, and your heart's huge. So I'm sure it just expanded with more people around."

"Maybe," he said cheerfully. "Now how about you go sit out on the deck, and I'll bring you a cup of coffee. And do you want some breakfast? Do you want something sweet? What can I get you?"

She shook her head. "I can't afford to gain any weight

while I'm here," she warned.

"Well, that's a lost cause already," he murmured. "Weight isn't even something I'm going to start with. You're hurt. You're injured, and your body needs adequate nourishment to heal."

She sighed. "But it's not time for the breakfast run yet."

"I do have fresh cinnamon buns," he suggested, wagging his eyebrows.

"Oh, really?" She pondered that for a moment. "How about half of one because I want to leave room for real breakfast food too."

"That's a good idea," he stated, with an immediate head nod. "I'll go grab that for you. You just find a place where you're comfortable, relax, and I'll be back in a couple shakes." And he was gone.

She pushed her way out onto the deck, absolutely loving the fresh air and the sunshine. It truly was a beautiful morning, even if she herself didn't feel all that optimistic. She would have to call her assistant to put off some of her work for the next few days. Because, if she were here, no way she would work her regular schedule. She was pretty darn sure Shane would kibosh that idea right off the bat. And probably give her a stern talking to about how much time she was spending at work versus resting and recuperating and doing some strength training.

It's not that he would be wrong, but she doubted that he particularly cared about the level of related problems she would have at getting her life back. Especially keeping her career. Of course she had chosen to complete her law school after much hemming and hawing, and now she wasn't so sure she'd made the right decision. Yet she had no clear childhood dream pointing her in any other direction.

When her phone buzzed with a text, she quickly read Shane's words.

Going to be here longer than Monday, kiddo. Get used to it. I need more time to confirm with another doctor or two here, plus to put together your rehab plan. I'll get back to you as soon as I can. Meanwhile rest up.

Hearing footsteps behind her, she affixed a grin on her face and waited to see Dennis walk toward her with a cup of coffee and a small plate. "You know that I … I understand how you have a lot more to do than look after me," she noted gently.

"There's nothing I wouldn't do for a longtime friend."

His voice was so gentle that it almost brought tears to her eyes.

Dennis continued. "And you were here when we had a lot of challenges, so don't go telling me that I don't have time to bring you something so simple," he explained. "And a lot of people are working here now, including Ilse, who would like to see you."

"Is she here?" Quinton asked in delight. "You know what? You make friends, and then life gets busy, and it seems like you just can't get back to all your friends anymore," she explained. "And then my brother was causing trouble here, and I felt like I should be apologizing instead of visiting with people."

Dennis burst out laughing. "The only problem your brother is causing is with himself because this is an opportunity, as you well know, that he's walking away from."

She agreed wholeheartedly, but getting her brother to understand that was a different story. "He did come see me last night. I think it shook him."

"Good," Dennis replied, without repentance. "He needs to be shaken. He needs to have some of that mind-set shifted, so that he isn't quite so difficult all the time."

"I'm really sorry about that," she told Dennis. "It never occurred to me that he would make life so difficult for you guys."

"If we can't handle your brother, we shouldn't be in business," he said. "So don't you worry about it."

She smiled. "That doesn't mean everybody's going to feel the same way," she noted, with a smile.

He just waved his hand at her. "Stop worrying about it. We deal with a lot worse than him here. I just feel sad for his sake, when I know there's so much benefit that he could learn from being here. But healing starts with him."

"I know. And I'm not sure whether my relapse—or whatever you want to call what I'm dealing with right now—has shaken him in the right way or made him wonder if any of it was worthwhile, because, well, *Gee, look at that?* I'm right back here again."

Dennis's expression revealed patient understanding, as he studied her gaze. "And I get that. But let's see what's wrong. Let's see how we can get you back on your feet, and maybe your brother will see your good example, and maybe he'll straighten up and fly straight. Two birds, one stone."

And, with that, he took off running back to the kitchen.

STAN WALKED TOWARD the entrance to his clinic from his nearby onsite apartment. But, even as he walked into the reception area, his mind was on Quinton. She was a special person, and he'd been trying to figure out how to take the next step. He knew he still loved her—in fact, he seemed to love her more, if that were possible—but the logistics of having a real relationship this time around seemed almost impossible to do when he was even more tied to the vet clinic than ever before. Just as she was more invested in her career.

He should have done something about it when she was here those eight or so years earlier, but, at the time, he'd been more concerned about not overstepping his boundaries by getting involved with a patient from upstairs. Now it seemed more acceptable, a trend Dani and Aaron had started. Stan had to chuckle at that.

So he and Quinton had stayed in touch, and, even though both were in the same geographical area, time seemed to be their greatest enemy.

Or maybe it was a lack of true communication? his mind nudged him.

Regardless, it had seemed like their relationship had grown more distant, and that was too bad because she was a very special person, and he really appreciated so much about her. But convincing her of that, after having let all this time go by, well, that wouldn't be so easy, whether dealing with an attorney or not. Stan felt it was more about being a man and a woman and letting her know just how he felt. Which scared him more than anything—that fear of rejection by Quinton.

So, if he was making excuses, he knew full well it was because it was easier for him to *not* do something than it was to do something and fail. He didn't really want to do the whole failure thing.

And that was hard to admit because, well, if he didn't try, he couldn't succeed; and, if he didn't try and succeed, he'd always wonder if he could have done something more to win over Quinton. And, of course, he already knew there was much more he could do. She was it for him. She was worth all the risk. He should have done something about it a long time ago. And now that she was here, he promised himself that he would.

At the same time, he was a busy man too. And that was only proven out as he opened up the schedule for today and winced. It would be a very long day. He'd be lucky if he had a chance to eat, much less do anything else, like have a heart-to-heart with Quinton. He also knew that he had to pick a good time to share his feelings with Quinton, to open up that dialogue to see how she felt about him.

Stan knew she was in pain, knew she was worried, knew she had a lot more health issues to deal with. All over again. He wished he could help her through that, but he knew that the human patients upstairs had to be the most engaged ones in their own healing.

Stan could help her, but Quinton had to do the heavy lifting. So he didn't want to burden her with sharing how he felt about her, until it was the best time for both of them.

Shaking his head, he put on the coffee, realized he needed to get some sustenance before his full day started, and he raced up to the dining room. Once there, he snacked on a cookie, while he waited for the hot food to come out.

As soon as Dennis saw him, he pointed out on the deck.

Stan raised an eyebrow. "What's up?"

"Quinton's on the deck."

He stared at him. "And here I thought she'd still be in bed."

"You knew?" Dennis asked him.

"Yes." He nodded. "I was here and heard about her collapse last night. Believe me. We're all terribly worried about her."

At that, Dennis nodded. "Me too, but she's out there with a cinnamon bun, waiting for hot food."

"Me too," he noted. "Any idea how long?"

"We're a good five minutes behind schedule," he replied, "so take your coffee outside and visit."

Well, Stan certainly didn't need any second urging to do that. As he walked outside, to give her fair warning, he called out and asked, "It's a beautiful day, isn't it?" It sounded banal to him too.

But now that he realized she was staying, and he had another chance to try to forge those bonds that he had let weaken, he felt his nervousness taking over. She twisted and winced. He raced forward. "Good God. I didn't think. Don't turn. Don't try to do anything."

She laughed at him. "It's my fault. If anybody should have remembered the pain involved with moving, it's me. But, of course, I completely forgot." She gave him an eye roll.

"How did you sleep?"

"Actually I slept really well. Shane gave me something for the muscles, and I have to admit it's been pretty decent, as soon as I crashed."

"Now that is good news," he said, "because you know how important sleep is."

"I'm not looking forward to today though," she replied in a low voice.

He sat down beside her, leaned forward, and asked, "Hearing the test results? Having Shane put you on his schedule again?" When she remained quiet, he added, "What's this hesitancy about? Do you feel you did something wrong?

"Not in one sense," she said, "I don't think so, but I'm afraid now I haven't been doing *anything* right."

"And there is a distinction," he admitted, "but you also know that they care and that they're here for you."

"I know. I know. I just … I …" She shrugged, gave him half a smile. "I'm worried."

"Of course you are," he agreed, "but you'll be just fine."

She smiled. "You always were such a great cheerleader." He winced at that. "Is that not a good thing?" she asked curiously.

"I don't know," he admitted. "I've never been called a cheerleader before."

"Well, it certainly wasn't meant in a negative way," she shared quickly.

He chuckled. "Hey, whatever way you want to call me, it's fine," he noted. "And I will help you in any way possible. You know that, right?"

She smiled and nodded.

"No, Quinton, I mean it. You need something, then you call me. Will you promise me that?"

She sighed. "If I can't get help otherwise, I promise I'll call you."

"Sneaky lawyer talk is what that is," Stan teased.

Quinton laughed.

"But I've got a pretty packed day downstairs"—and he wagged a finger at her—"which doesn't mean I can't help. I may just have to make a call or whatever. But I'll be by your side whenever you'll have me. So, on that note, I'm waiting for food to-go now, hoping that today would be one of those days where I get out early. Then I'll come check up on you."

"Sorry." She winced. "I know those days too."

"Too many of them, from the looks of you."

She sighed. "And I guess that's what I'm afraid is going to be the outcome of this."

"You mean, a career change?"

"I was trying not to say that out loud," she joked.

"Well, if it's killing you …"

"I hope it's not killing me," she stated, and then she withdrew ever-so-slightly. "But I will deal with whatever the message is."

"Good." Stan nodded. "Your health comes first."

She smiled at him gently. "And you," she added, "need to look after yourself because you do a vital service too."

"I do provide for the animals, but I'm often reminded of how very different my service is to them," he murmured.

"Don't let it diminish what you do," she repeated immediately. "For anybody who has a furry family, the job you do is something that none of us can do without. It would be just too heartbreaking to lose the pets we love so much."

Stan nodded, giving a quick chuckle. "I'm forever bringing in extra animals for people here to interact with. The minute everybody sees them, they fall in love. Now we have more service animals at every turn."

"And that's the way it should be," she agreed. "There's enough love to go around. We just have to remember that, and our furry friends help us to do that."

There came a whistle from behind him.

Stan stood and said, "Looks like there's food." He frowned. "Can I get you something before I go?"

"Nope, I'm just content to sit. You go. You're in a rush." When he hesitated, she smiled. "Remember? I'm here for a bit now. So we can visit later."

"Great. I'm looking forward to that. Dinner?" he asked,

as he backed away. "I don't know when or if I'll get time for lunch."

"Dinner it is," she replied, with a smile. "Although there might be a few other people joining us. Just because I haven't seen so many people in such a long time."

"I got it. Just include me in on the fun."

"Promise," she said, and he took off heading to the buffet line.

As he loaded up and picked up an extra sandwich to take down for his lunch, Dennis looked at him and asked, "Another bad day in store for you?"

"You have no idea. I'll be in surgery for most of it."

"Well, if that's the way it is today," Dennis noted, "make sure you take extra."

"This *is* extra," Stan said, with an eye roll. "If I keep eating like this all the time, I couldn't even waddle my way back up again from downstairs."

"Ha. I hear so many people complain about me trying to make them fat." he replied. "When the truth of the matter is, most of us here are losing weight."

Stan frowned, as he studied Dennis.

Dennis nodded. "I've lost ten pounds." And he patted his slim, long, and lean build.

"I don't know how you did that," Stan noted. "I'm not going close to a scale." And, with that, and a cheeky grin, he took off running. It would be a long day, and the sooner he got started, the better.

Chapter 4

LATER THAT MORNING Quinton made her way back to her room, now with a full stomach, and she felt her nerves kicking in. It took about twenty minutes of that same nerve-racking waiting before Shane popped in. She smiled at him.

"Hey," he asked, "you ready?"

She shook her head. "Nope, absolutely no way I'm ready. But I'm game," she replied. "So I hope you'll take that instead."

He chuckled. "I do remember that attitude," he noted, "and it is quite refreshing in so many ways. We'll start with getting those X-rays done and a physical evaluation and all that good stuff first."

And it took hours.

At least it seemed like hours. No, by the time she checked her watch, she realized it really had been a few hours, and she was exhausted.

Shane slowly wheeled her back to her room. "Now it's eleven-thirty, grab a nap, and then some lunch."

"I didn't want to eat too much at breakfast," she admitted. "I was worried about pain and all that was on tap for today."

"It's never a bad idea to tailor your meal consumption with what your day here looks like," Shane agreed, "at least to control the food a little bit, in case the stomach revolts."

"It never really was an issue for me to have a revolting stomach," she said, "but I sure didn't want today to be the first day either."

"Understood." He nodded. "I'll be back in a little bit. I've got appointments, and I'll go over all the results from your tests and then probably talk to a few doctors." He lifted a hand, as he left her room.

"Got it." She struggled to stand, feeling her good leg trembling. Shane's physical exam was a workout in itself. He hadn't worked her too hard; *she* had pushed too hard. She'd always had a problem understanding when to stop. Today was no different. As she leaned against the bed, she looked at the bathroom, the wheelchair, and then the bathroom again. It would be both easier and more difficult to get there using that chair.

Glancing around, she found her crutches against the visitor's chair. "Drat," she whispered. They were just out of reach. But then that seemed to be her life at the moment—everything was just out of reach. Using the bed, she hopped forward, feeling her good leg protesting each movement. Grimacing, she reached the crutches, propped them under her arms, and headed to the bathroom. It was a small triumph.

But she'd take it today. Actually she'd take it any day.

STAN WORKED THROUGH the day, trying hard to stay focused. But inside was this inner light of knowing that he would see Quinton again. Honestly, he felt like a schoolboy again. Which was both unusual and exciting, while completely nauseating. Because the last thing he wanted was for the same insecurities and the same hateful doubts to rise up. And yet, to be honest, had there been anything but doubts over the past many years, would he would have done something about furthering his relationship with Quinton?

And somewhere along the line he'd decided that he probably wasn't a good match for her or that she wouldn't want him. And maybe he'd just been so busy that he'd pushed it off and ignored it all. Whatever it was, he had another opportunity to get to know her a little bit better, and he was more than excited about it.

He grabbed his phone, sent her a text at 3:30 p.m., letting her know that he had another hour, if she was still okay to wait on him for dinner. He got a response back almost immediately.

I'm resting but missed lunch, so the earlier, the better, but okay to wait a bit.

He sent back an immediate response, setting it up for five o'clock. He hated that she'd missed lunch. Was it because she was exhausted from the testing? He didn't know, but he knew that Dennis wouldn't have been very happy with her either. She would likely get a mouthful from him when she finally got to the dining room. But maybe not.

Stan pondered it throughout the rest of the afternoon, and, by the time five o'clock rolled around, he was out of the office faster than he had been all week.

His assistant grinned at him. "Got somewhere special to go tonight?" she teased.

He winced. "Is it that obvious?"

"Absolutely." She laughed. "And I'm so happy for you."

"Ah, don't," he replied. "I've known Quinton for years, since she was first here. It's just …" He shrugged. "I was so busy, and she was so busy that it didn't seem like it would work out or was the right time, or I don't know. I've been trying to figure out exactly why I thought that I needed to wait back then."

She smiled. "Sometimes things have to happen in their own time frame."

"I agree with that completely. Right now especially. And, while I hate it that she's in pain and back here again to deal with health issues, I'm delighted that she's close by. So we're going to have dinner together," he shared, a boyish grin on his face. And, with that, he dashed out the door.

"Good luck."

He just raised a hand. Everybody knew that he didn't date much since starting this clinic, and he spent all his time with the animals. He really needed more help. Thank God that Aaron would be here eventually. So many people had asked Stan several times if he needed to find a life without the animals. The answer had always been: *Nope, not going to happen.*

But, as he raced toward his dinner date, he could just hope that Quinton felt well enough to keep their dinner plans. And he'd have to be gracious and understanding if she didn't. He could even arrange picnics in her room, if needed. That would go down well for him too. Feeling like an idiot and unable to stop these thoughts, he tried to slow down his speed when he got closer to her room.

Sure, he couldn't stop helping the animals, being a veterinarian. Yet he would like to have a worthwhile personal life too.

He knocked gently on her closed door, and, when he heard her call out from inside, he turned the knob and stepped in. She was alone, which was another good thing.

Her face broke into a small smile. "Hey there, stranger," she said gently. "I'm glad you're here. I'm starting to fade away to nothing."

"And I tried to get here so fast," he replied apologetically.

"No, I understand, and believe me. The animals come first down there."

"And yet they can't all the time," he added. "We have to look after ourselves as much as we have to look after them." He pushed the wheelchair closer to her. "Shall we?" She nodded. He stepped over and gave her an arm. She slowly pulled herself up, and he watched the pain whisper across her face. "I'm sorry," he murmured. "It looks like you had a tough day."

"Somewhat," she admitted, with a sigh of relief as she settled into the chair, "but I'm determined to make it down for food. I'm definitely on the hungry side."

"I'm sorry you missed out on lunch too. How did that happen?"

"Because I fell asleep," she confessed. "And, when I woke up, I didn't feel well enough to go down and ask for food."

"You're going to have to get over that independent streak of yours pretty fast too. Next time call me," he protested, staring at her. "Remember. This place isn't just for new patients but for our friends who have further needs."

"I thought I'd left as a success story," she murmured. "It's kind of hard to realize that you aren't the success you thought you were."

"Absolutely you are," he stated firmly. "Don't even start down that road of a self-defeating attitude."

She burst out laughing. "Is that what I'm doing?" she asked in a teasing voice.

He grinned at the sound of her laughter, nodded, and added, "Definitely. And I understand. I really do. Some of this stuff is pretty darn hard to deal with. But other times it's much easier, so hold on. And we'll get through some of the tough times, and then it'll be easier after that. I'm here for you, Quinton. I mean it. Truly."

"Have you ever had a crippling physical injury?" she asked him curiously. He looked at her in surprise. She shrugged. "You've always been so very understanding."

"I think that's because I work with animals that are constantly dealing with physical injuries, which are really hard on them too," he suggested. "The worst thing is when they give up. There's almost nothing I can do to bring them back once they've chosen that route. It's as if they have this mental checkout. And they're gone. I can do all in my power, but I can't bring them back, nor can I get them to change that attitude," he admitted. "That's when it's really hard—when it's something that you can fix, but you caught them just a little too late."

"Well, I'm not even close to giving up, and I'm not even close to checking out," she declared. "So you don't have to worry about that part with me. I'm happy to have some help to get back on my feet and to be fully functioning, though."

"You got it. Whatever you want, whatever you need, you just have to tell me. Okay?"

She tilted her head, smiling at him.

"I mean it, Quinton," he said, harsher this time. "You help others so much, and now it's time for some of that to be doled out to you. I want to help you through this. Now did you contact your office?" he asked, as he pushed her wheelchair from her room.

She nodded. "I've canceled my appointments for the

next few days, and my assistant is trying to reschedule them all or see if someone else can appear in my stead. Any future appointments are going to be pushed off maybe a month, if I can get the clients to agree. My office sent me a bunch of work to do from here, which I may or may not do," she admitted, with an eye roll.

"If Shane finds out, you can give up on that idea."

"Isn't that the truth," she agreed, wincing. "He won't be a happy camper if he finds out the amount of work they sent me either."

"Do you have many current cases right now?"

"Not going to trial soon—thankfully," she noted. "And I haven't really been doing the type of work that I hired on to do either. We had a bunch of people leave, and we had all kinds of problems with staffing, so jobs were shuffled around," she explained. "Honestly, I've been rethinking what I want to do."

"Of course you have," he agreed. "Nothing like readjustments in life to find out what's really important."

"And finding out what's *really important* isn't necessarily what you *thought* was so important," she noted. "I still want to do an awful lot with my life. It's a matter of finding something that I can do to pay the bills, that makes me happy, and that still allows me the freedom to do other things."

"When you find out what that magical thing is," he stated, "please share with us because you never know. A whole pile of us may want to jump on board."

With that, she burst out laughing. "Oh my, if you had to leave your animals for even a few minutes," she said, "I think you'd be absolutely devastated."

"I don't know about that," he replied. "What I am is exhausted, looking forward to having Aaron here," he murmured. "He'll give me much more help in the clinic, and I can step back a little bit, take a breather, and see what's next to be done. Right now it's just go-go-go-go, and I don't get a break. He comes back on his holidays and helps out for a while, but he's still got a bit longer to go before I get that full-time assistant."

"And that will be really nice for you," she noted. "I know that Dani is looking forward to having Aaron around full-time too."

"Of course, yes, and the two of them are a great couple," he said warmly.

"And it seems," Quinton added, as she looked around, "that an awful lot of couples are happening here. That really surprised me."

"So many." Stan nodded. "So, so many. Back then it was different, all prim and proper, stricter rules. Plus, just so much was going on while I got busy downstairs building my practice," he shared. "So I followed the rules, never really socialized too much, brought up the animals to visit with our human patients, helped everybody along a little bit. Then all of a sudden *love* started happening, and now it's like, *Okay. Somebody changed the rules.* And they forgot to tell me."

She smiled. "And I'm sure it didn't take you very long to figure it out," she teased, with the gentlest of smiles.

"I don't know," he said. "Sometimes I think I'm still trying to figure it out." He gave her a bashful grin. "But now, milady, it's time for our dinner." He motioned toward the big dining room doors. "Any idea what you'll have?"

"I know the menus are on my iPad, but I haven't been looking at it," she admitted. "So I have no idea what's even offered for dinner."

He grinned. "Neither do I. Shall we find out together?" And, with that, they entered the dining room.

Chapter 5

Q UINTON WAS PLEASED at just how helpful everyone was. Stan rolled her into the dining area, as other people had been busy opening doors, stepping out of the way, and helping them along. Apparently Stan also garnered a lot of respect here, and, for that, she was happy for her old friend. As she got closer and closer to the buffet, she told Stan, "There are tricks to carrying trays—whether in a wheelchair or on crutches—but I never really was very good at it."

He chuckled. "Tonight you don't have to carry your own tray. I'm here."

"And who's going to carry yours then?" she asked, with a note of humor.

But Dennis heard her. He popped his head over the glass case and said, "Me. Me, me, me," and he held up his hand, like a schoolboy looking for a treat.

"*You*," she said, with a big grin, "don't need extra work from anybody else."

"It's not work," he argued. "It's being of service, and the people who don't recognize that being of service to another is actually a joy that we can share are missing out on so much."

And such sincerity was in his voice that she had to stare at him. "You know that, in some ways, you're a bit of a relic."

He laughed. "In all ways," he agreed, "and I know it, but

that doesn't change the fact that, if we can do something to make another person's life easier, there's no reason we shouldn't be doing it."

"Maybe not," she admitted, "but I don't think the rest of the world would agree with you."

"Isn't it a good thing that I'm not part of the rest of the world?" he teased, with a shrug. "I'm part of this Hathaway House world. And this world is where we all try to help each other. Now dinner? And, by the way, where were you for lunch?"

She winced. "I knew that you would call me on that, but the truth is, I fell asleep."

"And afterward?" he asked, his eyebrows shooting up. "You really haven't eaten all day, have you? You know what Shane is going to say when he finds out."

"Shane is going to give her a talking to," said Shane, from behind her.

She went to twist around and then hesitated and replied meekly instead, "Hi, Shane."

"You could have asked for a food delivery, you know? That pride and stubbornness of yours won't take you everywhere."

"No, not everywhere I want to go, apparently," she confirmed, "but I knew I was coming here for dinner, and I wasn't terribly hungry earlier. Plus, my stomach was still not too impressed, so it's all good that I waited."

"It is, as long as you promise to eat tomorrow," Shane stated.

"I promise." She looked over and saw beautiful filets of baked salmon. "Oh my, I so want one of those."

"Done," Dennis said, with a big smile.

And by the time they were seated, their table had grown

by many people. Some she knew; some she didn't, but all were friendly; and all were jovial. She looked over at Stan, who sported a big smile and appeared to be enjoying himself. A part of her wouldn't have minded a quiet dinner with just Stan. But this place? This was all about acceptance. And she badly needed that.

She looked over at Stan and whispered, "This was a great idea, thank you."

He nodded. "How about breakfast tomorrow, just the two of us?"

She nodded, and her heart jumped.

THE NEXT MORNING Stan woke with a smile on his face. He'd had a wonderful time the previous evening, and it seemed like she'd thoroughly enjoyed dinner, and so had he. He hadn't realized just how many friends he had here at Hathaway House until he started naming them all for her.

She also knew a bunch of the people here, but she didn't know everyone, and it was such a joy to see the acceptance on everybody's face as Stan had introduced or reintroduced them to her. A few people were looking for an explanation, but also a few were just completely happy to see that they were gathered here and spending time together. Nobody made any rude comments or joked in any way that embarrassed her, and that was important too.

Stan didn't know what he and Quinton had together—didn't know that *they* had anything. He was hoping that they did, that it was more than one-sided. What they needed was time.

After dinner, when he'd taken her back to her room,

she'd looked quite wiped out. He worried about her all night and had even waylaid Shane this morning, asking if she would be okay. Shane had reassured him in generic terms that she would be eventually, but that it was early days yet. He wasn't still fully convinced about what had gone wrong for Quinton and what would be entailed to put Quinton back to rights, if indeed that could be done;and that had not been good news.

At the same time, Shane was a good person, a qualified physio. He was on her medical team, so Stan had to trust him.

And next he went to Quinton's room and wheeled her to breakfast. They ate out on the deck again, just the two of them. "I'm being selfish, but I like having you just to myself for a meal."

"Me too," she agreed. "We always did get along, didn't we?" she asked him, serious, staring into his gaze.

Stan nodded, gathering up his courage.

"And it feels like we resumed our relationship, like we just left it yesterday," she added.

"You are so right. That's exactly how I feel. It seems like our time apart didn't stop what we have."

"And what do we have?" she asked, again with that direct stare of hers.

"I think we have something great, something we should continue, but this time we need to have real discussions, I think, to share our feelings more."

She frowned. "Real discussions about what?"

"Your hopes, dreams, fears, wishes. Even discussions about what we're all told not to speak of."

She gave a brittle laugh, putting her hand to her heart. "Like what?"

"Politics, religion, money, sex." At that, he waggled his eyebrows at her.

She burst out laughing about that. "Okay, I can handle that."

"Good."

"So you want to get to know me better?" she asked.

Stan smiled, nodded. "Yes, ma'am. I want to know all about you."

Then Robin appeared by his side, announcing, "We have an emergency downstairs, probably a surgery."

With that, Stan touched Quinton's hand and said, "To be continued. I'll have Dennis get you back to your room."

Before she could argue, Stan took off with Robin.

Stan worked through the morning, and, at lunchtime, he raced upstairs, hoping to catch Quinton. But, when he walked into the dining room area and didn't see her, he walked up to Dennis and asked, "Has Quinton been here for lunch yet?"

Dennis immediately shook his head. "I'm afraid she's crashed again. And she's too polite to call and get something delivered when she needs it."

"I know for sure that she won't accept help, no matter how many times I try to convince her otherwise. And I fear she feels like a failure for having to return here—even more that she may think that she is taking a bed from somebody else," Stan suggested in a low tone.

Dennis winced. "Of course she does. I've seen it many times. She figures that she's had her time and now doesn't deserve it anymore. And that's pretty rough too because people who were patients here previously can still need help afterward."

"I know she's got a few days off work, but I don't know

how long she can stay here because, like the rest of us here," Stan noted, "she has a full-time job and a career that she struggles to get back to."

"I wonder how much she enjoys that career," Dennis said. "Sounds like it's pretty stressful."

"It's very stressful for her, and she mentioned she's considering her future work options. Yet she has no clue what else to do."

"Just like everybody else here at times," Dennis agreed, with a glance behind him. "Nobody here has easy answers in that department. If she looks deep enough, I'm sure she'll find something."

Stan walked to her room but found no sign of her, so that was a surprise. When he heard voices, he looked over to see her in the hallway in her wheelchair. He walked toward her and noted she was talking to her brother. Stan stopped and hesitated, not sure he wanted to interrupt them. Her brother had a bad rep at the moment. Stan didn't know whether or not Ryatt had improved enough to get over himself.

It was tough in a place like this because everybody knew who the troublemakers were, and you didn't really want to be labeled one of them either. Then again Stan didn't know the cause of Ryatt's behavior, and, in this place, that could be anything. But, as Stan waited for Quinton to look up and notice him, Ryatt saw Stan first.

Ryatt motioned behind her and said, "Looks like Stan's here, waiting for you."

Immediately she pivoted in her wheelchair, her smile breathtaking when she saw him. "Hey, I was hoping to head down for lunch, wasn't sure what you were up to."

"I checked in the dining room for you first. I didn't

mean to interrupt you." He motioned to her brother, who was already turning away and heading down the hallway. "Does he want to join us?"

She turned back, frowned, and then shook her head. "No, I did mention it earlier, but he isn't quite ready."

"Is he ever going to be ready?" he asked in a low tone.

"I don't know," she replied softly., "I keep hoping so. Right now he's going through a rough time."

Stan loved the fact that she understood where Ryatt was coming from. "It's not easy for anybody being here."

"No, and I'm not finding it easy being here again either," she murmured. "I feel like such a fraud. It's such a weird feeling because it's not something I ever really thought about before. But because this is such an important part of so many people's lives, I just feel like I'm taking something away from others. I already had my chance."

"Just because you had one chance," he argued gently, "doesn't mean you don't get a second chance."

She looked at him, smiled, and nodded. "That is a lovely way to put it," she murmured. "I can't say I was thinking about it in quite those terms."

"They have made it very clear that you're more than welcome to be here and that they're working on a treatment plan for you," he stated. "So I really don't think that you need to worry about being here."

"So why do I feel bad?" she asked, as they slowly made their way down to the dining room.

"I don't know," he replied. "Maybe you should answer that question yourself."

She looked up at him and shrugged. "It's never quite so easy."

"It never is," he murmured. "We know that, but, at the

same time, it's up to you to figure it out too. Everybody here just wants the best for you."

"And I know that," she said, with a gentle smile. "And it's appreciated. Everybody here's been wonderful."

"That's good because you know that they would all feel terrible if they knew how you felt."

"Well, it's … it's so hard," she shared. "I was doing so well."

"And you will again," he told her immediately.

She frowned, as if afraid to face him, and asked, "And what if I don't?"

"Ah," he murmured. "Fear raises its lovely head again."

She winced.

"Right?" he asked.

Quinton paused. "What … I mean, what if I don't improve? What if I don't get better again? What if this is where I'm at, and what if there's been some breakdown somewhere along the line, and I just won't go back to the way I was?"

"And maybe you will," he suggested, "and maybe you don't *want* to?"

Startled, she looked at him. The double doors to the dining room opened ahead of her. "What do you mean?" she asked. "I'm not *trying* to be in this wheelchair."

"And I'm not saying that at all," he replied instantly. "I'm just wondering if you want to go back to the same job, the same type of work you did, and deal with the same kind of stress. I highly suspect that stress contributed to where you're at right now."

"That would be a very tough move, if I did choose that," she murmured. "I do think sometimes about changing my career, but that's not an easy adjustment either."

"Sometimes the good things aren't easy—but that

shouldn't discourage us from doing what's best for ourselves. Like, with your current profession, you're a lawyer, but can't you do different kinds of lawyer things?" he asked, with a shake of his head. "And I guess that probably sounds pretty foolish, and I don't really know what I'm saying, but surely you can practice in other areas, right? I mean, something of your own choosing?"

"Maybe I could." She shrugged. "Obviously there are other specialties. I just ... I mean, I never really looked at it *for me.*"

"And maybe it's time for you to think about *just you*," he noted. "So how hard a thing would it be for you to do this? To switch areas of law?"

"I don't know how much trouble it would be. Different areas of law are governed by different rules," she murmured. She looked around, smiled, and added, "Being here does give one a different perspective, and it does remind me just how lucky I am. I mean, I have most of my body parts," she said, with a chuckle. "And most of what I'm missing isn't necessary."

"Are you missing organs too?" he asked.

"I lost a lobe off the liver, and I lost my spleen," she shared. "A chunk of my small intestine but not a big piece. They managed to patch that back up again. So, all in all, I'm doing very well. It just doesn't feel like that at present. ... And I think maybe you're right. Maybe it's the fact that I'm suddenly now in a very stressful job again, and it doesn't look as if there'll be any improvement in the immediate future."

"And that can be a huge hindrance to your healing, both mentally and physically, as well as emotionally," he noted. "Just think about it. It's not that you can't do something, but it makes it hard to imagine doing anything different."

"And yet maybe I need to."

"It's definitely something to think about," he suggested. "I'm not trying to tell you to change your profession. I'm just saying that you should consider where your stress levels are at and how you can minimize that."

"Noted," she said, "and thanks. Thanks for looking after me."

And, with that, they moved into the dining area. As they walked in, Dennis looked up, smiled, and greeted them. "Good, I'm really glad to hear that he found you."

"Yep, he did, indeed," Quinton said. "I was trying to convince my brother to come down, but he's avoiding the dining room crowd."

"Yep, he's got some issues to deal with first," Dennis noted.

"I know. I know," she agreed. "I don't know whether my being here makes it worse or better."

"Well, he hadn't made very many close friends even before you got here," Dennis murmured.

"Maybe, but, if he has a problem with me, then he has to open up and actually talk to me," she stated, "and so far he's not."

"And he might not be able to yet," Dennis reminded her. "Do you remember when you first came here?"

She frowned, shook her head, and asked, "No. Was I terrible?"

He laughed. "It's not that you were terrible," he stated, "but, like your brother, you couldn't very easily discern your emotions and decide what it was that you wanted to do here. Plus, communication was a tough two-way street," he stated honestly. "And we don't blame you or any of the other patients for that because, as you know, the adjustment period is pretty rough, as you all start that long process to healing."

"I was a mess," she agreed. "You guys were all pretty new. I was one of your first patients. It was ..." She shook her head. "It was hard all around."

"That it was," he murmured. "All around. But, like us, you survived and thrived," he said, with a big smile. "And that's what you have to hang on to."

"I get that. It's just sometimes ..."

"Like now," Dennis added, "don't look at this as a setback. Look at this as a change—a chance for you to make a decision about how you want to move forward."

"If it were that easy," she stated, "I would. I just don't think it's that easy."

Chapter 6

QUINTON HAD A lot to think about, just from her most recent conversations with Dennis and Stan. Not easy stuff either. And Shane gave her a lot more when he sat down with her and discussed her health and her healing.

"I have a plan, but it's going to take a few weeks."

She winced. "I don't think I can stay that long," she murmured.

"I guess the real question is," he added, "can you afford to *not* stay that long?"

She stared at him, silent.

"I'm not sure the job you're doing is terribly good for you," he shared, "but I leave that up to you. But something that you've been doing, the injury to your leg, the actual way that you're standing, has caused all kinds of nerve damage and incorrect muscle alignment, and we must get that fixed."

"And how do I do that?"

"It will be an intensive couple weeks to start with," he explained, "and then, depending on our results, I hope at that point you can go to outpatient status."

"So I need just two weeks off?" she asked hopefully.

"Three weeks *might* do it," he murmured, "but honestly, I would much prefer to have four weeks to work with you."

"And do you think I can stay here for three to four weeks?" she asked. "Is that even fair?"

At her last question he stopped and looked at her in surprise. "Fair in what way?" he murmured. "Fair in the sense of you having a bed that you think might belong to somebody else?"

She winced. "Does it seem that obvious?"

"Absolutely. You have to remember," Shane stated, "that you're just as important as the next person."

"But I've already had the benefit of everything here," she murmured. "How can I ask for more?"

"Well, one, you're not asking. We're offering," he explained. "Two, as I told you earlier, we're doing an outpatient program—specifically for people with recurring problems. And, three, I don't think we can do what you need in an outpatient program yet," he forewarned her. "Maybe in the next three weeks we can do it, but I won't know until we get you into this next part of your rehab. That's actually one of the questions that I have to take a look at and see just how you'll handle it. Give me at least two weeks," he offered, "and then we'll take another look." He asked, "You have any days off coming?"

She nodded. "I do."

"Might be a good time to request those."

"And theoretically," she shared, with an eye roll, "I'm supposed to have some medical leave."

"Well, you know what? If there was ever a time to request that," he said, "it would be now."

"Let me talk to them," she murmured.

He smiled and added, "How about you don't talk to them, but you tell them. Tell them what you need in order to continue to be a healthy, functioning individual."

"I'd love to, and I guess that's really what it's all about. I've been so worried about getting back on my feet again and not losing my job in the meantime."

"How much of your fear"—Shane held up a hand to stop her from arguing at his word choice—"is because you have deemed yourself as not whole."

She stared at him, her shoulders sagging. "Probably too much," she murmured. "How do you ever get over that?"

"Have you ever been treated differently because of your prosthetic?"

"They don't necessarily know about it at work," she admitted. "I always wear pants, and, of course, it's not obvious then."

"So, if they don't know, do you think that they are treating you differently? Or do you just fear that they're treating you differently because you feel differently, that you consider yourself not whole, that you're not enough. Therefore, you're not good enough, and thus they won't want you."

"Wow." She gulped several big breaths of air, his insights hitting her hard. "Feels like you're reading my mind. ... And I guess those thoughts are part of it," she murmured.

"It's not mind-reading. It's just human nature. I've been doing this for years. And this exact problem comes up more times than I would like. And my answer is always the same. Why don't you work on that while you're here too," he suggested. "You're here regardless. You might as well do as much as you can. You know that we have great psychologists on staff. That hasn't changed."

She thought about that and smiled. "You know what? I *could* do that, and you're right. If I'm going to be here for a couple weeks, I might as well make the best use of it."

"Exactly," Shane agreed. "Make the best use of it, get as much of the negative stuff worked out of your system as you can." Then he smiled. "And I know Stan is more than happy to have you close by."

"He's a really sweet man."

At that, Shane stopped and looked down at his clipboard, frowning.

"What?" she asked. "What are you frowning about?"

"So tell me. Does *sweet* mean you like him? Do you like him as a man, or do you just like him as a friend?"

She felt the color washing up her face. "Does that matter?" she asked softly.

"I think to Stan it matters a great deal. Maybe think about that. Now we'll start your workout, and we'll get you realigned and show you where you've been getting off track. And I'm sorry, but these next couple days are going to be hard."

She frowned and nodded slowly. "Okay, let's get to it then."

In the back of her mind was always his comment about Stan. Yet one hour into Shane's rehab workout, her mind was drained and empty, her body covered in sweat. She discovered not so much pain but a deep sore ache from holding herself wrong for so long. The muscles had been compensating, and Shane was gently getting the blood circulation back to those affected nerves. "I know the workout's almost done, and that's a good thing, but I don't think I can do anymore."

"I suggest the pool," he said.

"I'd love to, but I didn't plan to be here, so I don't have a bathing suit. I never thought to ask for such a thing when requesting a bag of personal items and clothing from home," she admitted."

"I know we keep some on hand," he told her, "but I have no idea if something's there that you could wear. I'll send one of the women down to talk to you about it." And, with that, he disappeared.

She struggled, crawling to her wheelchair, pulled herself up, and had just barely collapsed into her wheelchair, gasping for breath, when one of the nurses stepped in.

She smiled at her and asked, "What size do you wear?"

"An eight."

"Let me go see if we've got something for you. I'll meet you back at your room." And, with that, she turned and disappeared.

Quinton slowly rolled her wheelchair down the hall back to her room. She hated this absolute bone weariness inside, detested the fact that she recognized it all over again—also noting that never-ending work ethic that Shane instilled in her. But somewhere, somehow along the line, she'd forgotten about doing some of these exercises. Life had just gotten so busy, and she appeared to be fine, so she had not bothered. And she was ashamed to admit, apparently it was a failure on her part. And to find herself right now in this situation was just painful, both mentally and physically.

When the nurse returned, holding out several bathing suits, Quinton looked them over and said, "I'm almost too tired to get changed."

"I can understand that," the nurse agreed gently. "You don't have to go to the pool, but you might want to remember just how good it feels to sink into that water and let your body just cool off."

Groaning, Quinton nodded. "Like Shane told me. I'm only here for a few weeks, and I need to make the most of it."

When the nurse left, Quinton got changed, put herself into the wheelchair again, and slowly, too slowly, she moved to where the pool area was. As she came poolside, she locked in the wheelchair, and grabbing the railing, got up on her one foot ever-so-slowly and hopped the few steps to the edge. She didn't try for grace. She didn't try for form. She didn't try for anything except to reach the water. As soon as she got close enough, she tilted forward, until she fell in, the cool waves washing over her.

HIS HEART IN his throat, Stan watched from the stairs as Quinton got into the pool, hating to see the pain and agony on her face. He kept willing her to make one more step that would get her to where she was going. And when she crashed into the water, such relief and joy were on his face. He wanted to jump up and down. He also didn't know if she would even welcome somebody witnessing her struggle.

For a lot of people here at Hathaway House, it was hard for them to let others see how weak they had become or how different physically they were now than what they had been in their prime. Like now, she had only her one leg, and she didn't have her prosthetic on, and her body looked shiny with sweat. Stan figured Shane probably had done a heavy workout on her.

And she looked beautiful to him.

When he looked around for other witnesses, Stan found Shane leaning over the edge of the upper deck of the outside dining area, watching her too. Stan noted the relief on Shane's face too, that she'd made it safely into the pool.

Stan walked up the stairs and stepped up to the deck of the dining room, where Shane was. "Was she allowed in there?"

"Yes, but she was supposed to wait for somebody," he noted.

"Did you have those rules back then?"

"We didn't have the pool back then," he added, with a side grin. "Thankfully she made it okay. But I'll have a talk with her about the protocols."

"I don't think she did it on purpose," Stan replied immediately. "I think she was just exhausted, and she really fought to actually get to the water."

"I know," he agreed. "She'll feel better in a few days, but the next couple will be rough on her."

"I don't know whether I should stay out of her way then," Stan mentioned, "or make an extra effort to come by and let her know that she'll get through this."

"I don't know either," Shane admitted. "It's obvious you care a great deal for her."

Stan flushed. "I always did, even when she was here last time. I let her slip away and go on with her life. At the beginning of Hathaway House," he said, "we were all experimenting. We didn't have a set workable plan. We didn't have the routines set. It was live and learn as we went."

Shane nodded. "I remember, and you're right. It was pretty chaotic in those beginning days of Hathaway House, and we learned by doing things, both the right way and the wrong way."

"Do you think I'm hurting her chances of healing?" he asked.

"I don't think so," Shane stated. "I will tell you if I see that happening, and I know that your heart is engaged with her in a big way. You might want to see if your feelings are returned equally by hers before you get your heart too entangled."

"It's actually too late for that," Stan admitted, shuddering. "It would be nice to know that I was on the right track, but I don't have that reassurance to date. Yet I have decided that it would be now or never because I let her slip away last time, and I won't be repeating that mistake."

Shane nodded. "Good luck with that then. I love seeing the two of you together. You look really good. I'm not sure where her head space is at though, so choose wisely if you start an honest talk with her."

"Her thoughts probably aren't in a good place at all right now," he noted. "But when does anything ever come easy for us?"

At that, Shane laughed. "You've got the right attitude, if nothing else. And she is constantly looking to see where you are."

"I'll take that as a good sign," Stan said, with a smile. "I'm going to go down and talk to her, if that's okay."

"Absolutely it's okay. And she's going to need a reminder about time anyway. She's still on lawyer time and not on Dennis's time."

Stan smiled, as he shook his head. "What she needs is to get off lawyer time and to get into a job that won't kill her with the stress."

"I wouldn't be at all upset to see that happen either," Shane agreed. "She needs more physical activity on a day-to-day basis. Not sitting in a chair for sixteen hours at a computer, which is killing her neck and her spine."

"Yes, I'm definitely in agreement with you there." Stan nodded. "But telling her that and getting her to change? Well ..."

"Exactly. She's the one who has to decide. We can't

force her, not if we want the change to stick." The two men smiled in agreement.

Stan lifted one hand. "I'll see you at dinnertime." Then he raced downstairs to visit with Quinton.

Chapter 7

WHEN SHANE HAD warned Quinton that the next few days would be rocky, he hadn't been kidding. They were beyond rough; they were brutal. Quinton was in tears at night. She took anti-inflammatories to sleep. To keep her body moving, she was in the hot tub on a regular basis and in the pool just to keep things fluid. And still her muscles hurt. Not only did they hurt but they were sometimes agonizing.

Yet she understood why now, and, after having seen her muscles in action—although isolating the ones that she needed to utilize was a different story again—she was getting there. Some of the exercises were completely different from those she had learned last time. Either they were more advanced or her need was different. She didn't know, and so far she hadn't bothered even asking. She was too occupied trying to keep her head above water.

When she showed up at her one-week appointment with Shane, and, for the first time, she wasn't absolutely in agony. He watched as she rolled in, his gaze intense.

"Yes, I'm feeling better," she said, "but that doesn't give you a license to beat me up some more."

He chuckled. "Don't need a license for that. I already got one."

She rolled her eyes. "Well, it's the first time I didn't

wake up crying in pain," she murmured.

"I'll take that as a good start," he noted, "but it's not supposed to be so painful."

"It's not supposed to be, and yet somehow, with you, it always is," she muttered.

"And again it's not supposed to be."

"Good, maybe I can look forward to that one day," she murmured. "I've been doing your program for a week now. Do you see the results that you were expecting?"

He shook his head. "No," he stated bluntly. "Like I told you earlier, I'd need to see two weeks of your results at the very least to see how much longer you should be here. I'd like to have at least three weeks, maybe four."

She hesitated. "So I guess I'll talk to my office."

"You know that you should not be *talking* to the office but you should be *telling* the office, right?"

She smiled. "That's for people who are confident in their jobs and in the value that they bring to the company because they've already been shown that they have value," she argued. "Unfortunately that is not something I have available to me."

"And, if that's their viewpoint, that's their loss." He turned to face her. "But, if that's *your* viewpoint, that's a bigger problem."

"Yes." She waved away that second part. "However, it's also my paycheck, my income, and not all that many people are out there who will hire someone like me."

"And what does *someone like me* mean to you?" Shane asked.

She bowed her head to avoid answering him.

"Quinton?"

"Disabled," she murmured. And it took more out of her to say that one word than to do all Shane's tortuous rehab movements.

"I think you're wrong," he replied. "You may have a small handicap physically, but you have a bigger handicap mentally." When she frowned, ready to argue with him, he continued. "The next time you go to the dining room at mealtimes, I dare you to find any patient here right now that you would change lives with or just swap bodies with."

He might as well have slapped her, as Quinton reacted with a bodily jerk, and then she felt shame for not being more grateful, more thankful.

Shane nodded, watching the expressions on her face carefully. "But I understand that your mental insecurity is still a huge factor for you."

"Apparently, yes. I have gone to a couple sessions to talk it out. And I'm getting there. I'm just not there yet."

As they got back to work, he asked Quinton, "How's your brother doing?"

"Not as good as I would like," she murmured, "but he too is starting to open up and to talk a bit."

"I have heard from the other staff members that he's been a little more cooperative."

"I think it was a shock for him," she suggested, "to see me here."

"It's a shock for everybody," Shane agreed. "We all want to think that recovery is a one-time deal and that, when we're *fixed*, it's permanent," he murmured. "The thing is, everybody leaves when they get back to their new normal, yet improvements are still available over time. But that can also mean some problems are out there, ready to hit you too."

"And that, of course, is what happened to me," she said, with a nod. "Wouldn't it be nice if, just once, it would go our way and not against us?"

"And yet you just said that you're doing so much better."

"I am, indeed," she agreed, with a chuckle, "and that is thanks to you."

"Nope, not at all. None of this is thanks to me," he replied. "This is entirely thanks to you. *You* did this—not me, not Stan, not Dani. We gave you the opportunity to come back and to get realigned again and, while we'll be your cheering squad, it really isn't our doing. It's your doing."

"How about," she said, "it's a combo?"

"And that's possible," he admitted, with a chuckle. "Now, let's get started, so we can call it done, and you can go off and do whatever else is on your list of things to deal with."

"I'm going back to the psychologist today," she shared, wincing. "Sometimes those sessions are harder than any of yours."

"Oh, now my reputation's on the line." Shane waggled his eyebrows. "We'll make sure you work hard today then."

"Please don't." She groaned. "I take it back. I take it back."

But they were both laughing as they sat down and got started.

STAN HEADED UPSTAIRS two days later at noon on a whim. As he got to her room, he heard voices inside. As the voices raised in temper, he winced. He knocked on her door, hoping to stave off a full-blown argument. He wasn't sure who or what was going on in there, but he knew that Quinton didn't need any added stress. When there was a hesitation and then her voice called out, *Come in*, he opened the door and poked his head around. Of course it was her brother fighting with her. Stan glared at him.

"I'm not browbeating her or anything else."

Stan was stiff as he studied the younger man. "Maybe not, but, just like you need peace and quiet for your healing, she does too."

"I was trying to convince her to stay long enough to actually heal this time," Ryatt explained.

"That's good," Stan said, surprised, then looking over at Quinton.

She flushed. "I stayed last time until I was healed. Yet I don't think Ryatt has any business telling me what to do when he's not performing very well himself."

"That's hardly fair," Ryatt replied.

"Why?" she asked, glaring at him. "You think the staff like coming to your room or dealing with you? You've made everybody miserable even to be close to you. No, you're not the worst patient they ever had," she muttered, with a wave of her hand, "but how is it that you're even okay with being in the running?"

He flushed for a long moment. "Am I that bad?"

She raised an eyebrow. "Maybe you should take a look at your behavior and be the judge of that yourself," she snapped. She waved at the door. "Go on," she said.

He frowned. "Feels very much like you're dismissing me, like Mom," he replied in a mocking voice.

"I'm dismissing this whole event right now," Quinton declared, "because Stan's right. It's not what I need. It's not what I want."

Ryatt nodded. "Fine, but I'm not going to leave it alone. You should be here getting fixed up for as long as it takes."

"I am here getting fixed up," she muttered. "You don't see me packing to leave, do you?"

"No, but you were talking about it. About not being here next week," he stated, glaring at her. "They asked for two to three weeks to do the job right, and here you are at ten days, trying to pull out."

She glanced over at Stan and flushed. Stan immediately understood. "Maybe that's true," he admitted. "And I think she has a few lessons to learn about being here too."

"Maybe," she agreed. "Maybe we all do."

"Absolutely we all do," Stan muttered. "Doesn't matter if you're upstairs or downstairs, healing has to happen, and, if it doesn't, it's something that you carry with you for the rest of your life, having shortchanged yourself."

She sagged on the bed. "I also have to keep my job," she added. "And they're not happy that I asked for two weeks. Longer isn't possible."

"How long did they say you could have without it being an issue?" he asked.

"Ten days."

At that, his eyebrow shot up. "That's not even the bare minimum of the two weeks Shane asked for originally."

"I know," she stated, "but what am I supposed to do, lose my job too?"

"Well, if you can't perform that job," Stan noted, "you're going to lose it anyway."

"That's what I just told her," her brother snapped. He sat at the doorway and asked, "What's it going to take to convince you to stay here?"

"How about you having a change of attitude too," she snapped right back. "Do you think I want to be the sister of *that* patient?"

He flushed bright red and, without a word, turned and left.

She immediately groaned. "Is there anybody who can push our buttons more than family?" she asked, brushing the hair off her face. "I need to go apologize."

"Why?" he asked. "Didn't you mean it?"

"Yes, I meant it," she stated. "I've already heard it said behind my back a couple times, and it's pretty distressing that that's what I am known by, my association with my brother." She shook her head. "At the same time it's not fair to him because what I think and feel is not what should be affecting his decisions. He has to do what's right for him."

"And you have to do what's right for you too," Stan noted, with a nod of his head. "But it doesn't have to be exclusive of each other."

She groaned, then shook her head. "I'm really hungry, bordering on *hangry*."

"Let's go then. You'll feel better physically and emotionally," Stan shared. "I was hoping that you hadn't had lunch yet and that we could have a meal together."

"I haven't eaten," she confirmed. "I was just heading out to grab something when Ryatt arrived."

"Well, do you want to walk or ..."

"If I did walk, Shane would have my head on a platter," she muttered. She motioned at the wheelchair. "I'll go in that again."

"Good." Stan pulled it forward for her. "Let's go for a ride."

She laughed. "How come you're always in such a sunny disposition?"

"We're all in a sunny disposition, until we're not," he replied. "I'm older than you, and I've seen a little bit uglier times in life through multiple patients—animal and human," he noted. "We're not all so very different. When things are going great, everybody can smile and be happy. However, when things get tough"—he paused—"the inside person shows up. Same for your brother. And it's up to us how we want that inside person to grow and to change."

"And that's a wise viewpoint," she muttered. "When I was here before, I worked my ass off. I did everything I was told, and I worked hard. I always tried to be pleasant, always friendly and grateful, no matter how hard my recovery was. So I knew what a gift this place would be for Ryatt's soul and his health," she explained. "And I guess I feel like my brother doesn't appreciate anything anymore. And that's because his attitude is, *The world sucks, and I don't want any part of it.*" Settling into her wheelchair, she looked up at Stan. "You don't think he's suicidal though, right?"

"I don't see that, but I'm not around him much. I would hope not," he replied. "But you know that we have seen many a patient here who has been. Maybe you could ask Dani or somebody? Even if they can't tell you specifically about his medical file info, they could reassure you that they are watching for something like that with Ryatt," Stan suggested.

She winced at that. "God, that doesn't even bear thinking about."

"No, it doesn't, but, for some people, these are life-changing injuries, and not everybody is completely happy to adjust to their new reality," he murmured. "And I, for one, can't judge anybody who's found themselves in that situation. Animals give up when they hit a certain point, and so do people. Whether we like it or not, our actions, everything we do, has an effect on our environment. And not always the effect we want it to. I know you would feel absolutely horrible if your brother wasn't here tomorrow, especially when your last words to him would eat away at you for the rest of your life."

"Which is why," she said carefully, "I want to go apologize."

"As long as you know what you're apologizing for," he stated, choosing his words equally carefully. "It's not that you should be apologizing for caring about how he handles life here but that you should apologize maybe—and I'm saying *maybe* because I don't know how much of an issue this all really is—that you were more offended by how your reputation and your status here would be affected by his behavior."

There was dead silence for a long moment, as Stan stilled her chair to a complete stop in the hallway. "That," she whispered, "hurts."

He winced. "I know, … but I wouldn't be a friend and somebody who's concerned about your own progress here if I didn't mention it."

"And that was always one of the things about being here," she admitted, "that I had forgotten. Just how blunt tough love is and also how broken we can feel over the simplest act. You're right. I had no business yelling at him because I was going to be the sister of somebody who was *that* patient."

"And yet, being in that position," he added, "is also affecting your progress."

"It shouldn't though," she stated. "It's not his problem. My status, my view, my healing is not his problem. His problem is his attitude." She groaned. "And I didn't see that before. Why didn't you come along five minutes earlier, before I made a fool of myself?"

He laughed. "I wish I could have, but maybe this is by far the better way. At least this way you can be honest with him when you talk to him again."

"He's not going to want to talk to me for a while," she murmured. "And why would he? That was a pretty bad thing I said."

"At the time you were hungry, tired, worn out, also stressed. It hasn't been an easy day for you, and I don't think in any way he's even considering the fact that, for you, this isn't an easy time either."

"No, I'm sure he isn't," she muttered. "We never like to consider what other people are going through."

"Nope, not usually," he agreed. "Now can we go on to lunch?"

She shrugged. "I don't think I can eat anything now."

"You want to talk to him first then?"

She groaned. "I don't think he'll want to talk to me yet."

"But you won't know until you try," Stan suggested.

"Agreed." She brushed her hair back again. "I should have just had a shower and stayed in my room."

"And what would that have done for you?" he asked. "Outside of the fact that you would have broken my heart because I didn't get to see you over lunch."

At that, she stopped, stilled, and looked at him. "Shane said something to me earlier—not today, not even sure when it was, maybe a couple days ago. And I didn't know what he meant. And I'm just starting to get an understanding."

Stan froze. "Oh?"

"You know that I can't stay here all the time, right?"

He nodded immediately. "Of course I know that. We all want you to heal, to return to your life, hopefully your new and improved, less-stressful life," he noted.

She hesitated. "That's good to hear."

"Okay, is some disconnect going on here? What am I missing?"

"I just don't know," she began, "that I can be what you want me to be."

"Ouch. Sounds like it's our day for hard truths. And is this because of what I just said?"

"I hope not," she said, "because that would make me feel even smaller and more useless than I had originally. And, no, it isn't. I don't know what I want. I don't know what I need. Apparently what I said wasn't good for me or for my brother or you either," she admitted, "so now I'm kind of lost."

"Do you want me to leave you alone?" he asked.

"Yes."

"For how long?" he asked.

She never replied.

Probably for the best right now. The hurt behind that one word hit him hard. It was his own fault; he had presumed they had something more than they had, when he hadn't actually checked in to see if she was there on the same level with him. And he should have. He made an assumption, and he already knew how terrible those suckers were.

"It's obviously not a good day for you, and maybe we should put off discussing some things until later down the road," he offered, trying to give himself some distance from the crushing pain. "I'll go grab something and head back to work." And, with that, he bolted down the hallway.

He heard her calling him, but he just … He couldn't. Nothing inside him would let further injury to his heart happen. Even that kind of emotional pain was something he hadn't experienced in a very long time. He completely eschewed the option of lunch and instead headed downstairs, going back to work. When he popped in the office, his receptionist looked up at him, smiled, and asked, "Did you miss out on lunch, or was the service that fast?"

"I didn't get a chance to make it there. I took one look at the line and left."

"Oh, *ugh*," she replied. "It's funny. Some days I can't handle a line. Other days, it's not so bad."

"If you go later to the dining room, can you grab me something too?" he asked. And, with that, he walked without another word into the back area. He closed his office door, sat down at his desk, and hated, absolutely hated the fact that he felt tears pricking the back of his eyes.

That was not how he wanted to go through life. His phone buzzed. He looked at it and noted it was Quinton. But he didn't dare answer it. Not only would she hear his choked voice but he didn't want to listen to any insincere apologies. *God, was there anything worse?*

He took a long breath and released it, got up, did several yoga stretches to try to calm his mind. He had a busy afternoon, and no way any of his patients should have to pay because he was an idiot. A lovesick one, yes, but still it all boiled down to the same thing.

He was an idiot.

And, with that, he forced himself back to work and the one thing that made sense in his world.

Chapter 8

TO SAY QUINTON had never done anything so regrettable as she had today was to put it mildly. She couldn't even eat. She'd gone to the dining room, not knowing what else to do, knowing that her body desperately needed sustenance, but she didn't have anything to give; she didn't have anything to offer anyone. When she sat in her room afterward, she made a few simple clicks on her tablet and canceled all her medical appointments for the rest of the day.

Stan wouldn't talk to her; she knew that. She didn't even know what she wanted from him. And why had she said what she'd said? Was she still being so petty that she had lashed out because of his criticism? God, what did that say about her?

He was a good man, and he'd been a great friend. But she'd held everybody at a distance, incapable of handling what was likely to be a relationship that would go nowhere. Every time she tried to get close to somebody, once they found out about her prosthetic and her injuries, it all blew up.

She didn't even know why it was such a big deal. It shouldn't be a big deal, but apparently it was a big deal. And yet obviously it wasn't a big deal for Stan; he dealt with things like that all the time. He also knew her from before, so he was fully aware of her prosthetic and her other injuries.

So why had she lashed out? And, of course, the answer was there in her face.

She'd lashed out because she was insecure and hurting, and, in so doing, she'd done nothing but hurt him. Feeling very small, very upset with herself, she decided that, if he wouldn't talk to her, then maybe she could heal the one other relationship where she had caused so much pain. So she headed down to see her brother. He was in his room, getting ready for his next session.

He looked up and in a casually indifferent tone asked, "What do you want?"

"I wanted to apologize. Your healing needs to depend on you," she stated. "I was wrong to make it seem like it's all about me."

"It's always all about you," he replied. "That's the joy of growing up with siblings. You'd say it's all about me, and I'd say it's all about you." He shrugged. "Most of the time it's not an issue. Now that we're both here, well, maybe it is."

"Do you want me to leave?" she asked bluntly.

He moved closer and looked at her. "Didn't I make it clear that I want you to stay and to get better?" he asked. "You've always put everybody else first. When are you going to put yourself first? When are you going to listen to the doctor and take care of business?"

"I haven't always put everybody else first," she argued. "I was here for months before."

"Sure, when you were physically incapable of getting out of that bed and had no job with cruel bosses demanding you get back to work before your doctor says so," he reminded her. "There was only so much anybody could do to help you, but, once you did get to that point of independence, there was no stopping you," he said. "Once you saw success, once you saw change, you were off and running."

"Of course I was. I was taking up a bed from somebody else. The same as I am now."

"You're taking up a bed because *you* need it right now," he said in exasperation. "Stop making this about other people. This time you need to make it about you."

She stared at him in bewilderment. "Maybe I'm just dense, but I don't understand."

"Just one time, you need to stop trying to always be perfect, stop always trying to be better than, stop always trying to be the answer to whatever it is that everybody else seems to need," he explained, "and maybe, for the first time in your life, do something for you. In this case, it means telling your job to stuff it. You need this time, and, with any luck, you'll be back to work in a few weeks."

She stared at him, mute.

He looked at her and sighed. "And it's a good thing you've got friends here," he added. "That's something that most of us have to build once we are here," he murmured. "Stan is seriously hooked on you, and you're so lucky because somebody cares, even though you got a prosthetic leg. He doesn't see it. He just sees the woman he knows from years ago and finally has a chance to get to know all over again," he noted. "Don't mess it up, sis."

She winced. "Too late," she said bitterly. "I already did." And, with that, she pushed from his room and slowly rolled back to her room, tears streaming down her face.

STAN WORKED LIKE a fiend for the next few days.

Finally Robin stopped him. "Stan, I love you to bits. I

don't know whatever it is that's driving you, but it's going to kill you," she said bluntly. "Please find a way to get an outlet other than your office, other than your work, to let go of some of this."

He just stared at her, not liking that she'd even broached this topic in the first place.

"I get it. I see it all over your face. *Don't talk to me. Leave me alone. Everything's fine,*" she stated with emphasis. "But it's not fine, and we all know it's not fine. We don't know what's wrong, but we can guess," she added gently. "Is that what you want us doing? Because the human psyche will say that we're looking for answers to fit your behavior into some kind of explanation that makes sense to us."

He flushed. "You don't have to say anything," he muttered.

"You're hurting. We get it. We don't know how to stop it. We don't know how to help you," she said. "And obviously we'd do anything we could to make it easier."

"It'll just take time," he stated.

"And I get that, and that's fine. We all need a bit of time sometimes," she agreed, "but maybe just remember my words. And, the next time you get ugly at somebody here or on the phone, just remember that we're all part of a team. Everybody is affected by everybody's behavior on that team." And, with that, she turned and walked out of his office.

Of course that made Stan feel even worse. Which was pretty hard to do, considering he already felt like roadkill. What was he supposed to do? How did one handle rejection like that? And why was it even such a big deal? Except it was because he thought Quinton was his one and only chance at real love. And apparently not only was Quinton *not* his one chance but she had *never* been his chance. They were friends.

He'd been friend-zoned.

He laughed almost bitterly at that. *It is what it is.* He needed to pick himself up and carry on.

WITH THAT MANTRA still beating in his mind, Stan headed to breakfast early the next morning. Dennis took one look and raised an eyebrow. Stan held up a hand. "Don't say it, please."

Dennis slowly closed his mouth, then asked, "What can I get you?"

"Something good, something hot, something filling," Stan replied. "I've been running on nothing for a few days."

"Yeah, I know," he stated bluntly. "You've hardly even been in here."

"No, I haven't been in at all," he admitted. "Some things take time."

At that, Dennis nodded. "Come on. Let's get you some sausages and eggs and something for the stomach acid to chew on instead of your soul."

At that, Stan grinned. "Now if only food were the answer for everything."

"It's the answer for a lot of things," Dennis stated. "The rest? Well, the rest takes time and healing."

"I've never been so great on patience."

"But that's not true," Dennis argued in surprise. "It's one of the things you do best."

Stan stared at him in shock. "What?" he asked. "We just hit a discussion I never expected to have."

"Maybe you weren't looking," Dennis explained. "Maybe you weren't seeing just what was out there, but you're an integral part of this community. If you hurt, everybody hurts."

Stan shook his head and laughed. "Not true."

But a soft voice behind him said, "It is true."

He turned to see Dani there.

She hooked her arm through his and patted his hand. "We love you, Stan. And when somebody's having a difficult time, we all just hope that you get over it okay."

"I'll get over it just fine," he muttered. "I'm sorry that my behavior has affected everybody." He was, in truth, a little on the bewildered side. He hadn't expected this kind of a response. He looked at her and added, "I'm fine, honest."

"No, you're not," she replied, "but you will be, and that's what we have to hold on to."

He smiled. "You know what? That's … That's kind of gold right there."

"It is." She chuckled. "And you'll get there, and whatever it is that you need to get out of this," she added, "you'll get that too."

"Thanks for the vote of confidence," he murmured.

"You know that we love you."

"I love you guys too," he said. "I was having a tough few days."

"Well, I'm not sure if it makes you feel any better—because you're not the kind of person to want to hear this—but she's not having a good couple days either."

He instantly winced at that. "Right, that whole guilt trip of hers working on overdrive."

"Is that what it is?" Dani asked, with a knowing smile. "I don't know that it's so much guilt as maybe that inability to have held back her words."

"I overstepped the line, and she put me back on my side

of the line quite clearly," he noted, "and it took me a few days to understand where I belong in all this."

"I don't think you understand where you belong at all," she replied. "Come on. Let's go sit down and just rest a bit."

"I don't understand what you mean."

"I think she regrets what she said. I don't think she believes what she said. I think she was hitting out. I'm not sure what the conversation was, before or after that scenario," she murmured, "but it's definitely affecting her."

"Of course it is, and of course I didn't even think of that."

"No, when hurt, we tend to lick our own wounds and don't necessarily look to see who else might be hurting," she explained. "And again that's not a criticism of you. When you're reacting, you react. It's only when you manage to get out of that reactionary episode," she said, "that you can get to a point where you see what else is happening around you and where you can start to care again."

He sat down in his chair with a hard *thunk.* "I feel like a heel now. I came up here thinking that I had it together and that it was safe."

"Love's never safe." She smiled. "The minute you risk your heart, you leave the safety zone."

"What happens when you get friend-zoned?" he asked, raising his tortured gaze to Dani. "How do you deal with that?"

"With grace," she said, "with compassion and understanding."

"Yeah, … I didn't. I didn't do so well in those departments. And I think I flunked them in school."

At that, she burst out laughing. "And keeping your sense of humor helps too," she added. "Something that you are well-known for."

"I don't know about that," he replied. "I've been burying myself in helping with my animals."

"And you know something? I'm not sure there's a better healer than what the animals can bring us."

Stan nodded. "It's been a good few days for me that way, and thankfully I haven't had too many hard cases which, you know, would have just made it all that much worse."

"And that's because you come from the heart, because every one of those animals is important to you. It's not a case of, *Oh, it's too much of a bother. Let's put them down.* You always give them that extra chance," she noted, "so I guess what I'm asking is, could you reserve judgment and give *her* a chance?"

He stared at her in shock. "You don't understand. She made it very clear to me."

"Yes," she replied gently. "And I don't know exactly what she said, and I don't know what it was that she *intended* to say because I'm not sure that those two things were exactly the same," she murmured. "I guess all I'm saying is, she's suffering far more than somebody who has just guilt."

"So I need to go let her off the hook, *huh?*" he asked. "I'm not sure I'm fortified enough to see her again."

"And you don't have to be right this moment," she stated. "Sometimes these things take time. But, when you are ready, you might want to put her back into the friendship space of your life. Because she was a good friend to you." She paused, gave him a gentle knowing smile. "I know. It's not always black-and-white here."

"It's never black-and-white," he murmured, "but it sure can be hard."

"It doesn't have to be. Sometimes it's easier. Sometimes

it's not, but I can tell you one thing. It's never boring."

He shook his head. "I was so happy."

"We saw it." Dani nodded. "And of course now we also see the devastation and the aftermath."

"I didn't really want my life to be so public," he said in a low voice.

"Not sure you can have that here," she added. "Everything's public. When I was struggling with Aaron, it was just as public. And I do remember you giving me many a hug because I was lost for a long time."

Stan let out a heavy sigh. "I had forgotten," he murmured, studying her carefully. She had been lost in such a way that he knew she now understood what he was going through.

"I hadn't forgotten. It's partly why I'm here," she explained. "You told me not to give up. And you were right."

"Yeah, but I was right then, and I'm right again now." He gave her a lopsided tilt of his head.

"That doesn't mean you're right about Quinton." At that she burst out, her laughter loud, strong, and incredibly infectious.

He felt some of the pain in his heart easing. "Fine. I will do my best to find a way to bring that friendship back online again because you're right. We were friends for a very long time."

"Good," Dani said, "my work here is done."

He snorted at that.

She hopped up. "If nothing else, I have to go back to work. The one thing that I do know here is one success breeds another, but something that absolutely never changes is how another person always needs help," she declared, "and I've got quite a few more coming in this week. So I'll love you and leave you." And, with that, she turned and walked away.

He sat here, eating his breakfast, wondering for a long time what he was supposed to do with Dani's request. It wasn't the easiest, and it sure wasn't out of line on her part either because he could see from others that this needed to be resolved, as it affected everyone here.

That was the problem with living in a fishbowl. Stan had never come up against it personally before. Had never thought that his love life—or the lack thereof—would ever fit this kind of a scenario. But obviously he had to do something about it for no other reason than his own self-esteem. Just as he was ready to stand and to head downstairs to work, he heard a voice behind him.

"May I sit here?" she asked.

He stiffened, didn't turn around. Of course there would always be the chance that he'd see her when he came for meals, but he'd really hoped that maybe he wouldn't. And now here she was. He pushed back his chair. "Sure, I'm done." And he was actually, so he got up. "It's all yours." He finally faced her and gave her a bright smile and left.

He'd take it as one little step toward regaining their friendship; it was about all he could handle. And he didn't dare turn and look behind him.

Because, if she was anywhere near upset, he couldn't deal with that either. And he strode quickly down the outside steps and headed back to work.

Chapter 9

QUINTON FINISHED HER breakfast and headed back to her room but knew that she had absolutely no constructive answer for what she had just tried to do. How did she attempt to build a bridge when nothing on either side existed to hold it? She'd heard from others, Shane especially, who was concerned about her rehab progress, given her problems with Stan.

Finally she'd broken down and asked Shane, "What difference does it make?"

And Shane'd turned on her and had let her know exactly what difference it made, how the entire community was affected when something like this went wrong. And it was up to the adults—and he'd emphasized *adults* quite harshly—to smooth things over so that there was at least civility.

Civility.

How could she have civility when her heart was breaking? And yet, from what she understood, it wasn't just her heart breaking.

Shane had told her, "I get you don't want anything to do with him on that level. That's fine, but you guys were great friends, and what a shame that you've lost that now too."

She didn't know how to tell him that she didn't know what she was feeling or how to deal with this. It's not a scenario that she'd ever found herself in before, but it was terrible. All of it was terrible. And it just made her feel even worse. She sat here this morning, alone, outside, eating her breakfast, wondering how she was supposed to pick up and fix this.

When she realized that really the best answer was to leave.

She didn't have to come back. Her brother was barely talking to her. She had always stopped in to speak to Stan, but she'd blown that now too. Swearing at herself, she pushed away from the table and headed back to her room. And Shane found her less than twenty minutes later, packing her bags, fully dressed, ready to check out.

He stepped into the middle of her room and looked at her. "Since when is running away an answer?"

She stiffened. "If there's no progress and no sign that progress will continue," she replied, "what's the point of staying here? I'm just taking a bed from somebody."

"You know what? I've heard that from you many times," he murmured. "Why is it that you think that you don't deserve the best of the best, the same as everybody else gets?"

"Because I had it once," she said, looking at him in surprise. "Why should I get it twice?"

"Why shouldn't you?" he murmured. "What's wrong with your thinking that only allows you one time to get things right?"

"A lot," she said in a sad voice. "And way too much for me to begin to talk about."

"So then, before you walk away," Shane stated, "I think you owe us a chance to talk to your psychologist here."

She immediately shook her head. "No, not going there."

"And I'm going to ask you as a friend and as somebody who stepped up and made sure that this bed happened so that you could actually heal and improve to the point where we could get you back on your feet." He faced her head-on, not letting her avoid him. "And, if after that session, you still want to leave, well, I won't stop you. We all have to make decisions in life, and we all have to decide how we'll go through life," he noted. "If you want to go through it running away, then that's your choice, your decision. Not mine."

"Wow, that's not exactly being nice, is it?"

"What you need right now is some tough love, not me *being nice*," he replied. "The truth hurts, and it's not just you who has to face that, so does Stan. You've made your feelings about Stan very clear," he said, "but that doesn't change the fact that we all still love you and that you still need help. So what's it going to be?"

She sank onto the bed. "Fine, I'll talk to the shrink. But don't expect it to change anything."

"I'm not expecting it to change anything," he shared. "After all, I see a lot of similarities between you and your brother." And, with that, he left.

If there was ever anything that would guarantee Quinton to be at a loss for words, it was a comparison like that. And she had to wonder, as she made her way down to her shrink session, why Shane would even say something like that. When she rolled herself inside, getting better at navigating doors and such in her wheelchair, Dr. Wagner looked up and smiled. "Ah, I heard you wanted to leave."

She winced. "Wow, everybody's just so involved in my business."

"It's part of being here, isn't it?" he asked. "You're part of a family."

"But it's not *my* family," she argued. "However, my own

brother doesn't want anything to do with me either."

"I think he does. I think he just doesn't know what to do with you," Wagner suggested. "So let's get comfortable and talk about it."

Quinton sat stiffly in her wheelchair, not sure what to say.

"I get it. You don't want to be here," the doc said, "but you did make an agreement with Shane. If, after the end of this session, you don't want to be here, then we'll all let you leave. I suspect we'll never see you again, which would be a shame for everybody here who has invested a lot of time in your care. But again that's your prerogative. We have that happen with people every once in a while."

"Do people really walk away?"

"Sometimes. Sometimes they disagree with the rehab treatment that they think they're getting," he shared. "Sometimes they think they're being taken advantage of or God-only-knows what. People can create all kinds of excuses in their head to make their decisions seem more plausible. And apparently you seem to feel that you are undeserving of a second chance."

"Why would you say that?" she cried out.

"I've heard you say those very words about yourself. And I see you acting out those words. Look at you," he began. "So many people have gone to bat to make this happen for you, and, even when this special opportunity is right in front of you, something inside you won't allow you to accept it."

She swallowed hard. "What's that got to do with a second chance?"

"What do you have against second chances?" he asked.

"I don't … I don't know," she replied. "I wouldn't have said I had anything against it." He just waited. "My mother.

My mother was very much like that."

"Well, then maybe we should talk about your mother."

"I really don't want to talk about her," she stated bluntly. "Any more than I want to talk about my brother."

"It seems like family drives a lot of issues for you."

She snorted. "There are a lot of issues in my family."

"News flash," he said. "A lot of issues are involved in everybody's family. Do you think anybody got through this journey called life without their own family issues?"

She raised both hands in frustration. "I don't know, but I'm barely holding it together right now. I really don't want to sit here and do a postmortem on my family."

"Where is your mother?"

"She's dead."

"Ah, that makes it harder too."

"Why?" she asked, looking at him. "It should make it easier."

"No, it doesn't," he countered. "We think it's easier because then we don't have to deal with it. But, in fact, it's harder because, at no point in time, do you ever get a chance to actually heal and to then move on. You're stuck in whatever land she left you in."

"A bad one," she muttered.

"How much did you have to do with her?"

"Not enough, too much." Finally she broke down and added, "Look. I don't know why any of it matters anymore because, like I told you, she's dead and gone. But my parents split up, and she didn't want me. She wanted my brother. I begged for a second chance, a chance to prove that I could be the daughter she could love, so that she would want me. But she wouldn't let me. Wouldn't let me. ... Wouldn't give me that chance," she said bitterly. "She took my brother and ran."

The psychologist let out his breath. "Did you hear what you just said?"

"No. What do you mean?" she asked. "What did I say?"

"You said that you begged for a second chance and that you couldn't get it. Your mother wouldn't let you have that second chance. And that is very much what's still driving you today. You don't think you deserve a second chance because your mother didn't give you a second chance—and obviously she was the be-all and end-all of your world back then. So you don't think *anybody* will give you a second chance because you're not worthy," he stated gently. "And you couldn't be more wrong."

She snorted. "Have you heard what I did to Stan? I mean, I'm *not* worthy. I hurt a good man."

"You can't control his feelings, and he can't control yours," the doc noted. "You are not responsible for what Stan feels for you."

"I've hurt him so badly. And it's not what I wanted at all."

"Good, then at least we know that you didn't do it on purpose."

She swallowed hard. "Please tell me that people out there don't do things like that on purpose."

"There are people out there," he replied, leaning forward, "that deliberately make people fall in love with them, just so that they can crush them. I've seen so much of life," he murmured. "I was hoping that wasn't what you were up to."

She immediately shook her head. "God, no, I would never do anything like that."

"Good." He gave her a bright smile. "That's very good.

Then I don't have to worry about that being part of this issue."

She stared at him in shock. "Why would anybody be so cruel?"

"Because they are hurting," he explained. "When people hurt, they lash out. Sometimes they don't know how to stop it. Sometimes they don't care to stop it. Sometimes they just want the hurt to go away. And yet they don't always understand what it'll take to make it go away."

"And you're talking about me now, aren't you?"

"Am I?"

Quinton glared at him.

He smiled. "If I am, you tell me. If I'm not, then you clarify."

"You're talking about me," she declared. "I hurt Stan terribly, and I … I still don't know why. Well, yes, I do." She stopped and let out another groan. "I don't deserve to be here. I'm a terrible person."

"Tell me why." Dr. Wagner leaned forward.

And she explained about the conversation with her brother and Stan's interference. "I … I didn't even realize how upset I was and how much it was building inside me, and, the next thing I knew, I was basically telling Stan that I didn't care about him and wouldn't ever care." The tears flowed down her cheeks. "I didn't mean to hurt him."

"And there's nothing like those we love who can hurt us the most."

"That's not fair," she muttered. "None of it's fair."

"Of course it's fair," the shrink replied. "It's all fair in love and war. And just as you have to deal with the onslaught of your emotions from your actions, Stan has to deal from the onslaught of his."

"But he didn't do anything," she wailed. "I don't even know that he does care, and why would he? I mean, look at me. I'm a freaking mess."

"Ah, we're back to that *you don't deserve a second chance.* And, of course, you don't believe that Stan should give you a second chance."

"Why would anybody?" she asked, staring at Dr. Wagner numbly. "I mean, seriously, why would anybody?"

"Maybe because you're a wonderful human being, underneath all that hurt and self-doubt," he replied in the utmost gentlest of tones.

She stared and shook her head. "And you're delusional. Didn't you hear anything I just said?"

"Absolutely," he confirmed. "I understand that your mother preferred your brother over you, that she took him instead of you, and that you felt like your life wasn't worthy anymore. Hopefully you found a way to let your father know that you still cared about him."

"I did," she answered immediately, "but life was not easy. He found a bottle, and that's where he stayed."

The doctor nodded. "And sometimes that happens, when you can't handle what's going on around you in life," he explained. "Sometimes the bottle is a lot more forgiving than looking in the mirror."

"Ouch." Quinton stared at him. "You guys really know how to hit hard, don't you?"

"And we're not trying to hit at all," he reminded her. "What we're trying to do is find a way for you to heal."

"It doesn't feel like healing is part of my life anymore," she admitted. "And I don't even know that I have that ability to heal."

"You do," he said gently. "You just have to forgive yourself."

"How do you forgive yourself for hurting people, hurting somebody who just made the mistake of caring about me?"

"First, you stop saying it was a mistake because I'm pretty sure Stan doesn't think it was a mistake."

"Well, if he didn't before, he sure does now," she stated bluntly. "You can't come back from stuff like that."

"And there you are again," the doctor pointed out. "You're back to that again. *I don't deserve a second chance.*"

She flushed. "Okay, so that little child inside me agrees. She doesn't deserve a second chance. Apparently she was so terrible that her mother didn't even want her."

"Or she was so wonderful that her mother was jealous and couldn't handle it."

She snorted at that. "You have no idea."

"You managed to stay in touch with your brother, I see."

"Not really, … not until I was much older. And I contacted him."

"So you really aren't close?"

"No," she replied, "and I wanted to be closer because, of course, I wanted to have that *whole family* thing, but, you know, it wasn't to be."

"And you *know* it wasn't to be?"

"Well, I mean, my brother and I stayed in touch. We were both in the military, but it's not as if we spent any holidays together, and I sure wasn't invited to my mother's house until much later. And only when she found out she had stage four breast cancer. She was gone within months."

"And do you have any idea what his life was like?"

She shook her head. "No, in my mind, it was the absolute best thing ever. Of course it was because it's what I couldn't have. And it's what I so desperately wanted."

"Does he understand how much your father leaving like that destroyed him?"

"Maybe, probably, I don't know. He may not even have thought of it."

"Do you not think that maybe he was as desperate to have his father as you were to have your mother?"

"And again I don't know. Both of them died not all that far apart," she added, "in an odd twist."

"I don't know about an odd twist," the shrink said. "Sometimes I think fate's like that. It's fickle."

"Yeah, isn't that the truth," she agreed sadly. She could feel every ounce of her just draining away into this gripping mud puddle of emotional sludge that she didn't want to deal with. Yet, as she sat here, she felt like … "It's the weirdest feeling," she shared, "but there's like a barrier starting to come down."

"I'd be very happy if there were a barrier coming down," he murmured. "It's a whole lot better than barriers going up."

She snorted at that. "I don't know." She shook her head. "It seems like it's all just so wrong."

"Maybe. Maybe it is all so wrong," he suggested, "and maybe it's just life. Maybe you just need to accept that everything isn't perfect and that some things in life just need to happen the way they happen."

She looked up at him, tears in her eyes, and repeated, "I didn't have to hurt that man."

"And now that you regret hurting him," the shrink began, "what is it you want to do?"

"I want to turn back time so I hadn't done that."

"Why? Because it's easier for you?"

"Right. So then I don't have to face the fact that he feels something for me that I wasn't prepared to face. *What did that say about me?*

"Interesting wording," the shrink noted. "Because you're not saying he feels something for you that you *can't* reciprocate. You're saying that he feels something for you that's happening at the wrong time."

"It's always the wrong time," she muttered. "I don't know what would ever make it the right time."

"How about maybe accepting that you're not perfect and that maybe you can't necessarily fix some things in life or make things perfect."

"I've always had to be perfect. Before my mother left, she told me that I wasn't perfect enough. I've spent all my life trying to be perfect."

"You've spent all your life trying to fix yourself for a woman who didn't care enough about herself to understand what was important in life, which was her children. And that woman is now dead, and you can't fix that either," the shrink stated. "So maybe you need a little bit of understanding in your own mind that some things just can't be fixed."

She didn't know what to say to that. She sat across from him, frowning. "I don't ... I don't even know what I feel anymore." Quinton raised her palms. "I'm so confused."

"Confusion's not bad," the shrink told her. "Out of the confusion should come some clarity, and, by the time you get home to your apartment, and you figure out what you want," he said, "maybe there'll be answers for you."

And that was the thing. He really was telling her that she could leave. "You're not going to stop me?" she asked hesitantly.

"No, heavens no," Wagner told her. "That's not my job.

We have a lot of people who want to be here. We have a lot of people who are here because they want to heal. I have no intention of keeping you here if you are an unwilling participant," he declared. "That doesn't sound like a good deal at all for anybody. And it would also ease some of the stress with everybody around because they're all so affected by it."

She shook her head. "I'm sorry. I didn't mean to make a mess of things."

"In what way did you make a mess of things?" he asked curiously.

"Well, you just said that everybody is so affected by it."

"Sure," he agreed, "but that just gives them opportunities to learn and to grow too."

"So am I supposed to go or not?" she asked in confusion.

He looked at her in surprise. "You tell me. I suggest you go back to your room and sit there for a bit and think about it. I do have another patient now, so let me know your decision—or don't." He shrugged. "I guess, if I see you again, I'll see you again. If not, I'll presume you're gone." And, with that, he led her to the door and put her firmly outside.

"I still don't know what to do," she cried out.

"You always know what to do," he argued. "When you don't know yet what to do, you need to take stock, take a moment and think, and then take a moment and feel. And remember. No decision, doing nothing, is still a decision. So, if you can't make a decision to walk out of here, calmly and quietly with confidence, then that's not where you belong." He added, "If you think that you need to return to your room and to think some more, then that's what you need to do."

"It's not that easy," she cried out.

He looked at her for a long moment. "It absolutely *is* that easy. You are worth a second chance." And, with that, he closed the door ever-so-gently in front of her.

STAN WASN'T SURE what was going on upstairs, but, when Shane showed up in Stan's office at the back of the clinic, Stan winced. "I know you're not down here to see if we have any more animals to bring up for your patients," he murmured. "So why are you here?"

"Partly to see if you're okay," Shane began. "You are a friend."

"I know"—he smiled at Shane—"and we will, all of us, get through this."

"Yes, we will. I just wanted to let you know that she's staying."

He stared at him. "I'm confused. I thought she was always staying."

"Actually she had her bags packed and was leaving."

He stared at him in shock. "What? Why?"

"Look. I won't get into her personal medical details, but, in the hopes of mending the environment here, I can tell you this. She didn't feel like she was welcome anymore," he stated. "Because, in her mind, she did something so terrible, so horrific, that she couldn't remain here anymore."

"Oh God." Stan felt each word like a hammer against his heart. "You know I never wanted her to feel that way."

"No, I know that, and inside she knows that too. But she's got some issues to deal with, partly with her brother, partly with her family, partly with just the fact that she won't ever be perfect."

"None of us are," Stan stated, moving his head back and forth.

"Nope, none of us are," Shane agreed. "But there's nothing that can twist us up more than hurting those who we love."

"What about her brother?"

"He's actually improving. He … As her behavior has become more difficult, her brother's has actually improved."

"Well, that's something," Stan noted. "They were having quite the fight the day I was there."

"We've all more or less pieced together what happened," he said. "And I think, after her brother got her good and agitated, then you may have just triggered something that set her off, and she spoke without thinking. Now she doesn't know how to get back to normal and feels like she doesn't deserve that chance to stay here and heal."

"Of course she does," Stan declared. "I never wanted her to leave."

"Of course not," Shane said. "And she probably isn't really thinking about leaving either. The bottom line is, I think she's working her way through it, and I don't know if you have the ability to step out of your comfort zone and to meet her partway and to find a way to be friends again or not. If you can, it would be good for both of you. If you can't, well, I tried." And, with that, Shane lifted a hand and left.

Stan sighed and sank back in his chair, then frowned. All his staff had gathered at his doorway, staring at him. "What now?" he asked, throwing up his hands. "It's been a really emotional few days."

"Oh, we know," they each replied, with an eye roll.

"Have I been that bad?"

"No," Robin said, "but we are all hurt because we know you hurt. And we all heard your conversation. Maybe close the door next time? Regardless, Shane's correct. We're family, and what happens to one of us tends to happen to all of us. And, if you can't find it in your heart to go out and to make peace with Quinton, we'll understand. We've all been there. None of us are judging you for it. We would very much like to see you happy, and, if it can't happen with her, then maybe it can happen with somebody better suited for you."

"You guys are way too understanding," he muttered.

At that, Robin smiled. "Not necessarily. We're just waiting for a chance to get back at you."

He burst out laughing, and they all grinned. "Fine, I'll try," he muttered. "I'm just not really good at this relationship stuff."

"Then take an animal with you," Robin stated bluntly. "They've always been some of the best ways that you communicate."

He raised both eyebrows and nodded. "You know what? That's not a bad idea. I didn't even get a chance to show her some of them."

By this time, the rest of his staff nodded and smiled, as they returned to work, leaving Robin behind.

"So maybe, on a friendship level, take that chance," Robin suggested. "And give it a try. You never really know what'll happen until you try."

He winced. "It really sucks though. You know that, right?"

"Yep, I do know that," she agreed. "One way or another, there's no true path in love."

"Doesn't even seem like there's *any* path," he replied in frustration. "I was so happy, and now I'm just, well, lost," he admitted. "I've been bolstering up my whole system to make it through the days and now? I … I don't know. I don't know what to say."

"And that's because," Robin noted, "there's just not a whole lot to say. If you're hurting, you know what you need to do. You need to grab an animal and find a way to not hurt so much."

He winced. "It's not that easy."

"Yes, it is. It's that easy to begin to feel better."

He groaned. "Fine, I will go make an attempt to see if I can fix some of this—but only on a friendship level."

"I heard what Shane said," she murmured. "You might want to remember that Quinton doesn't believe she deserves a second chance. And, if that's the case, she might not understand where you're coming from. On the other hand she might desperately need to know where you're coming from. So just be a little more open and a little bit accepting."

He rolled his eyes at that. "I'm not taking another hit in the head—the heart," he declared. "That was bad enough. I'm back, and it's where I need to be. And I get that, for you guys, this was a pretty rough road. And I'm sorry. But I won't go through that pain again."

"So you don't get a second chance either, *huh*? And you won't give her a second chance?"

He frowned and shook his head. "It's not that."

"It sounds like it's that," Robin stated. "And second chances are pretty important in our world."

He shrugged, not knowing what to say.

And she pressed home her point. "You're entitled to be upset. You're entitled to be hurt," she said. "Just remember to not hurt back. That's the animal in us, which lashes out, wanting to hurt anything and everything around us. But it's not who we are, and, once it's over, and you can see the pain and the ripples of pain, you know you feel like death warmed over."

"Well, maybe I wouldn't feel so bad, if maybe, for once, it wouldn't be that way."

"Maybe," she said cheerfully, "but I doubt it. You're a big softy. Whether Quinton knows it or not, you're all heart, and she's missing out on something very special." And, with that, she said, "I'll leave you with that. Sermon's over. Don't mind me. I'll just go back to work now."

And, with that, she walked away, leaving Stan to his thoughts. He listened, but everybody appeared to be silently busy. He walked to the outer office. "And, of course, you all agree."

As one, they all looked up and nodded. "Absolutely. We all deserve second chances."

"And what about my heart?" he asked in a tight voice.

"Noted. Understood. But you need to go try anyway," they all rushed to say.

He frowned. "So it doesn't matter if I'm hurting?"

"It does matter. It absolutely matters," Robin stated, the others nodding. "But it also matters what you do with it."

Chapter 10

WHEN QUINTON WOKE up the next morning, she still wasn't sure she'd made the right decision or not. But she was here, that much she had committed to. And yet the commitment itself had been so, so hard. She'd talked to several of her staff at work, and they'd all been extremely positive about her staying here—some even going as far as asking her what the other problem was that she would compromise her health at this point. She wasn't about to share her problems—with her brother or with her job—with her staff at work.

But then there was Stan. And that was something she would have to face, and it wasn't something she looked forward to, but it was something that she could not leave in good conscience without talking to him first. She'd never meant to hurt him. She wasn't even sure how she could possibly have been so difficult that she had done so. It wasn't like her. Or at least it wasn't normally her. But apparently she was a completely different person in that all-too-recent scenario.

She hated it.

The fact that her brother was here as well—to see her at her worst with him and with Stan—just added to the insult. It shouldn't. None of it made sense. She loved her brother, absolutely adored him. But it wasn't that easy to actually live with him. And she knew he knew that too. *I mean, how could he not?* It was a fact of life in a place like this.

At the same time she wasn't being all that easy on herself. That was really the lesson here—she needed to ease up so that she could actually be who she needed to be. And so she could stop worrying about how others looked at her and how others saw her. That was something that had taken her a long time to figure out when she was here the first time. She had that worry that people were judging her, were expecting her to be bigger and better and faster and stronger.

She suspected her brother thought that she would never be in this situation again, and he was down about it, not just for her sake but for his sake, because, all of a sudden, if she wasn't perfect and couldn't handle this rehab, then how could he?

Or maybe that's not what he thought at all.

Regardless it wasn't her fault if that's the way it was because nobody was perfect in this world.

Confused and tired, she stayed in bed, wondering if she even wanted to get up and go for breakfast. When a knock came at her door, she hesitated and then she called out, "Come in."

Dani poked her head around the door and looked at her, smiling. "I'm glad you stayed," she stated simply. "Remember. There's fresh coffee in the dining room."

"I was just wondering if I wanted to go down or not."

"Is *not* even an option?" she asked curiously.

"Maybe," Quinton replied. "It just seems kind of hard."

"Well, get dressed," Dani said, "and you can come down with me."

She frowned at that. "I don't really need somebody to walk me down there."

"We all need somebody to walk us down there some-times," she argued. "And, if you're thinking everybody here knows what's going on, you're wrong. They don't."

Quinton frowned at that too.

Dani laughed. "You're going to have wrinkles before you're forty if you keep that up," she teased.

"Like that's really high on my worry list."

"No, probably isn't, and that's a good thing," she noted. "We all know that these injuries play havoc with our physiological age too. But, more than that, it's the stress and the emotional trauma. You need to come down to breakfast."

Quinton groaned. "Fine, give me five." She shoved back the covers, as Dani stepped outside and closed the door. Quinton slowly got up, figuring out whether it was worth getting dressed or if she should just put on something easy to wear. As tired as she was, easy was probably the better way to go. But it didn't really sit well. She managed to compromise with a loose pair of pants and a T-shirt, and, when another knock came at her door, she called out, "Come in," to see Dani opening the door, standing there, waiting.

"Do you need help?" Dani asked her.

"I'm here. I'm ready," Quinton replied. "Sorry. Didn't mean to keep you waiting."

Dani shrugged. "In a place like this, we're always waiting on something," she noted, with a smile. Once Quinton was settled in her wheelchair, Dani pushed Quinton outside her room. Together they made their way down to the dining room. "How are you feeling this morning?"

"Like warmed-over death," Quinton replied bluntly. "Again, I feel like ..." And then she stopped.

"Don't say that you're not welcome here," Dani mur-mured.

"It's not the welcome. It's goes back to that deserving thing. I spent an hour on the shrink's couch yesterday," she shared, "and it wasn't an easy time."

"Never is," Dani agreed, "but more power to you for actually attending that session."

Quinton smiled at that. "He did give me a lot to think about, some stuff I hadn't really considered."

"He's good at that," Dani said. "They all are, actually. Even Dennis sometimes has the biggest pearls of wisdom, and I often stare at him because his whole outlook on life is so very unique."

"I wondered that too. He hasn't changed a bit," Quinton replied, with a smile.

Dani nodded. "It really is quite funny to realize just how brilliant he still is. I hope he never changes." She sighed.

"He's definitely got some special words to give everyone here," Quinton noted. "And yet he seems to be totally happy here, *huh*?"

"I've told him that, if he ever wants to change, to do anything else, to let me know," Dani added, "but he says nope. He's totally happy. And you got to love that because happiness isn't something that comes from outside. It comes from inside."

"Exactly, and he knows what he's supposed to be doing. And I don't really think he cares to be doing anything else," Quinton stated, frowning, wishing she had that in her life.

Dani smiled. "And we are blessed to have him."

"You are, indeed," Quinton murmured. As they made their way to the dining area, she sighed. "I don't even want to go inside because I'm afraid Stan will be there."

"And yet," Dani said, "you cannot spend your time here hiding away."

"Are you sure?" Quinton asked, with a teasing smile. "It would be nice if I could."

"Nope, not going to happen."

As they walked in, Quinton looked around quickly, but she didn't see Stan. She felt a sense of relief. "I hate to say it because I really do want to see him, but I guess I want to see him on my terms."

"Does that work for you often?" Dani asked curiously.

Quinton burst out laughing. "Right? It hasn't yet, so I don't know why it would now."

"Exactly," Dani agreed. "Maybe you should just forget about it and plan to have a talk with him when you get your head on straight."

"That's the plan." Quinton shook her head. "Doesn't necessarily mean it'll work out so well."

"Plans are like that," Dani declared. "Don't worry about it. Just one step in front of the other." By the time they had their trays full of food and made their way out to the deck, Quinton felt a little bit more settled.

She really had been afraid that she would see Stan when she wasn't prepared for it, and that just made her feel worse because it wasn't his fault. None of this was his fault; it was her fault. And the fact of the matter was, she didn't know why she had said what she'd said, and she didn't mean it, none of it, and she had to tell him that. "My day is full, so how would I set up to meet him?" Quinton asked Dani.

"Maybe you should call him, text him, say you'd like to have a few minutes and arrange a time."

"I suppose that might work," she muttered. "Does feel odd."

"Anytime you're in a scenario like this, it feels odd. Doesn't mean it's right or wrong. It's just different." She smiled.

"Yeah, you have a pretty interesting take on life too," Quinton acknowledged. "Not just Dennis, or Shane even, for that matter."

"I think life here gives us a unique perspective," she murmured. "There's always so much that we can't change or fix that sometimes you'd like to wring somebody's neck because they could be doing so much more, but, in their mind, they can't. And you know there's no reason why they couldn't except for those negative thoughts. Yet it's all stuff that we have to let everybody else figure out on their own," Dani noted, "just like you and Stan."

"Well, if there *was* a me and Stan," Quinton admitted, "it would be a lot easier. But having kiboshed that whole deal, I'm feeling completely wrecked about it."

"It's not kiboshed if you don't want it kiboshed," Dani stated. "Sure he's hurting. Anybody who took a direct hit like that would be hurting, but that doesn't mean that it's a done deal."

Just then another physio came and joined them. Soon a nurse joined them too. And very quickly Quinton was engulfed in the camaraderie that surrounded the place. By the time she was done with breakfast and slowly wheeled her way back to her room on her own, she had decided to take Dani's advice.

If nothing else, Quinton could text Stan and ask for a chance to talk. When she did get back to her room, she was just tired enough that she wanted to lie down. But first she sent a text to Stan, saying she just wanted a chance to talk with him.

She didn't get a response right away, but then he was probably in surgery. It was just one of those frustrating delays that now she would continue to check her phone to see if he had contacted her. Not that he would have or should have, just maybe that he could have. And, with that, and feeling a whole lot worse than she'd expected, she laid on the bed and waited for Shane, who was coming to her. When she heard a knock, she called out, "Come in."

And, sure enough, it was Shane. He took one look at her and smiled. "I'm glad you're here."

"You're the second one to tell me that this morning."

"Good, now believe us, and we'll all get along well."

She chuckled. "I'm working on it."

In a very serious tone he stated, "Work faster." Her eyebrows shot up, but he wasn't going there. "Let's go. We've got a full day's work ahead of us. You're pushing us on time to get you back to work," he said, "so we have to push you."

And what followed was one of the hardest days she'd had since she'd arrived. By the time she finished the session with Shane, she was shaking inside and out.

He looked at her, nodded, and said, "Now the pool."

"And if I can't even make it there?" she asked, gasping.

"Oh, you'll make it there," he stated, "because I can get you there, but I don't know about afterward." He frowned. "You may want to have dinner in your room."

"Yeah," she agreed, feeling the pain coursing through her, as she settled in her wheelchair. "I think you're right. I think the pool and maybe the hot tub."

"This is not necessarily an easy afternoon coming now either. I'll work you in the pool. There's no *easy* in this world. You know that." He pushed her out of the gym area and toward her room.

"Will you be deliberately hard on me?"

"Nope, but, with your work deadlines being an issue, I

don't have time to mollycoddle you. If we're going to get you back up and functioning at the level that you want to be at," he stated, "we have work to do. Your body needs some retraining to get it going in the way it needs to be."

"Got it," she said, still feeling the effects of this morning's workout, but at least Shane had pushed her chair back to her room. "Okay, give me five to get changed."

"I'll meet you down at the pool deck," he replied, and, with that, he was gone.

She groaned, as she closed the door to her room. She didn't have time to even whine about it, but, man, she sure wanted to. Changed, back in her wheelchair, and feeling the exhaustion leech through her soul, she scurried her way down to the pool.

She passed several people who were friendly but not anyone who she knew. Just a case of sharing space with them until she got where she needed to go. By the time she got there, Shane waited impatiently. She rolled up toward him and said, "I'm here."

"Okay, let's get you in the water." He helped her into the pool, and she just crashed, feeling the cool waves close over her head. She almost cried out in relief. Just something about having the water back in her world made her feel so much better. With his coaching, she quickly headed off and did a series of laps, and then she did a bunch of stretches and resistance exercises for her struggling muscles.

Of course they were struggling. She'd forgotten most of these exercises, if she'd ever learned them back then. When she finally caught a breath, she asked, "Did I actually learn any of this stuff back then?"

"Some of it's new," he replied. "I've been upping my training a lot myself. So it's possible a lot of this is new, but it's very relevant."

"I'm not arguing," she explained, "just trying to figure out how to incorporate some of this into a daily routine."

"And that would be something we have to work on too," he agreed, frowning. "It depends on how many weeks you're giving me here to get you back up to where you were before," he noted. "After that, it's going to have to be stuff you do on your own at home."

"You guys should do classes," she suggested, "for anybody who lives close who can come back and forth."

"There's a lot of things we should do," he agreed, with a headshake. "Just not enough time or not enough staff or not enough workout rooms." And, with that, he got her back to work again.

STAN GOT QUINTON'S text message, and he was surprised. Delighted, worried, but definitely surprised. He kept pondering it throughout the day. He didn't answer it though. It was really nice to have her close. But, at the same time, it also meant that he hated to come to work now. He didn't answer her text until later, and then, when he went to hit Send, he muttered, "This is ridiculous. I might as well just go talk to her."

Frowning, he checked at the end of the day to make sure all was well with the clinic before leaving. On the way out, he scooped up the huge bunny that was a service animal here. Hoppers should help break the ice. And then, taking a chance, Stan walked up toward Quinton's room.

As he wandered through the upper floor with the human patients, he stopped, spending a few moments with various people, as he let Hoppers hand out some of his beautiful healing magic. With his huge body and ears, he always got tons of attention. He was like forty pounds' worth of rabbit. Stan hadn't weighed him in a while, and he should because this was a seriously oversized rabbit.

By the time Stan made his way to Quinton's room, he was once again nervous. He knocked on the door awkwardly.

When he heard *Come in*, he frowned because it wasn't all that easy to face her again. A passerby laughed, thinking he needed help with the door, and opened it for him.

"Hey, that's one big load you got there," the woman smiled. "You almost need a cart for him."

He chuckled. "You're not kidding. Maybe a baby stroller." And he walked inside Quinton's room.

"Oh." She immediately flushed. And then she saw the animal in his arms. "*Oooh,*" she said, her voice instantly changing, softening. She sat up in the bed and held out her arms. "For me?"

"He's heavy," Stan warned.

She just wagged her fingers. "Gimme, gimme, gimme." She chuckled.

He reached over and put Hoppers in her arms.

She immediately buried her face along his neck and his big silky ears. "Now this is a bunny."

"Hoppers is on the giant side." And, indeed, Hoppers sniffled her face, his whiskers tickling her, his ears back, as she stroked him.

"He's so placid."

"Bunnies tend to be placid anyway," he noted, "but Hoppers is a special guy."

And then she realized the bunny was missing a leg. She frowned. "I guess he needs to stay as a pet."

"We can't let him go wild," he murmured. "Too domesticated."

"He means more than one simple meal for a coyote."

"A pack of coyotes," he noted, "and that's not the end we would want for this guy."

She immediately cuddled him closer. "He's beautiful." She looked up and smiled at Stan. "I'm glad to see you," she admitted. "I was waiting for your text."

He shrugged. "I went to answer it a couple times, but it seemed like I didn't quite have the right words."

She nodded in understanding. "I know. I've … I wanted to talk to you multiple times—but again trying to find the words."

"I'm working on it." He took a deep breath. "I'm happy to be friends."

"Well, that's good," she stated bluntly, "but I'm not."

He froze, feeling the air caught in his chest again. "What?"

"And again I'm not saying it very well," she added. "What we had before was more than friendship."

"But what we had before is not what you wanted," he stated equally bluntly, feeling the same pain again. He crossed his arms over his chest and glared at her. "You made that very clear."

"The only thing clear about what I said was the mud that I was slinging. And that is not me. I was having a pretty rough time with my brother. I was upset over the condition I was in and the fact that my job is not being very cooperative about letting me have time off," she shared. "And you just kind of hit me at the wrong time, and I took it all out on you."

"That's still just excuses for finally telling me how you

really feel," he muttered. But inside he seemed a little bit more hopeful.

"No, it's not," she argued. "That kind of behavior never has an excuse, and I'm sorry."

He nodded slowly. "Apology accepted."

They stared at each other, wondering how to get across this awkward moment.

He took a deep breath. "But I still don't know where that leaves me."

"The same as we were before?" she asked hopefully.

"But where was that?" he asked. "I find I now need clarification. You told me that what I wanted was not something you could give me."

"And I lied." And then she stopped, frowned, and added, "Maybe I lied. I don't even remember all the details on the conversation," she stated. "I know that I've done a ton of work this last week on my own personal self-confidence, and I've still got a long way to go."

"Something about not deserving a second chance."

One eyebrow shot up. "Are people gossiping about me?"

Such horror filled her voice, and he shook his head. "No, but this is your second chance back here again," he noted, "and a lot of people never even get invited the first time."

She winced. "Yes, that's part of it. The fact is, I am here on a second chance, and I haven't been fighting for it as much as I should. I should be telling my job to stuff it and that I'm taking this leave and that it doesn't matter what they think or not." She shrugged. "Apparently I have lost some of that assertiveness when it comes to my own income and a roof over my head."

"Are you that poor?"

She slowly shook her head. "I could afford to be out of

work for a few months," she shared, "but times aren't exactly easy. I'm helping my brother pay for this place," she noted. "And my uncle is struggling, so definitely some funds need to be funneled to him. So, if I go down, and I don't get a paycheck on a regular basis, everybody else is affected."

"And that's tough. However, Ryatt gets a pension, and he should get most of this stay here paid for."

"Sure, but you know there are always those extra expenses. And again I would be fine for a few months, but finding another job that would pay equally as well in this current climate, starting fresh with a disability," she added, "that doesn't appeal."

"How long can you get off on sick leave from your job?"

"I asked for three weeks. They said two, but I'm almost up to two, and Shane would like a couple more."

"Tell them you need three months," Stan suggested. "At that point in time they will have handed off all your cases, and, when you go back, you can start fresh."

She frowned, stared down at the rabbit in her hands, buried her face again in the middle of his neck.

Stan could see her warring with herself on it. "There is nobody more important than you when it comes to healing," he stated.

She flashed him a dimpled grin, and, of course, he was charmed all over again.

He sighed. "And I'm not going to tell you what to do," he stated. "You already know what you need to do. It's a matter of justifying it to yourself."

"Agreed and that in turn makes me angry all over again. I shouldn't have to."

"Of course you shouldn't have to, but that's life. So … decide what's best for you. It doesn't have to be what's best for others. Don't you know somebody who reuses a coffee filter to save pennies, but they'll buy something totally frivolous that means nothing to us but to them means everything? We all make choices, but, when you make those choices, and there's a limited amount of funds, you make sacrifices," he noted. "Maybe contact your uncle for an update on his situation. Explain what's changed in your world."

"That was part of the fight I had with Ryatt," she admitted. "He wants me to stay here and to get what I need to get done and to not help Uncle. He called our uncle and explained."

"Well, good …" Stan pondered her words for a long moment, then decided he needed to know. "As for us, I guess I would like to know a little bit more," he stated finally. "If you see me as a friend, I need to know that."

"Of course you're a friend," she replied in surprise. "I just said that."

"You mentioned a lot without saying anything," he stated bluntly.

She winced. "Yeah, that's the lawyer in me."

"Well, I don't do the lawyer stuff easily," he said, "so are we working toward more than friends or do you see me as a friend only?"

"I see you as more than a friend," she answered instantly. "Do I know what that is? No. Would I like to know what that is? Yes. Would I like to continue on this path, albeit a nicer path?" she asked. "Absolutely. Do I know what the end result is? No. Would I like to find out? Yes."

At that, he chuckled. "Okay, that was much better on the communication front," he replied. "That's starting to sound a whole lot more positive too." She gave him a beautiful smile, one that made his heart ache.

"I'm sorry," she whispered. "I really am. I figured I'd ruined everything between us."

"Let's just say it was an eye-opener to … to hear those words. And not in a good way."

"No, of course not," she agreed, "and, for that, I'm terribly sorry."

"You keep saying that," he said, nodding. "I will take this guy back down to his pen and, give him his dinner. What will you do now?" he asked her.

"That's a good question," she noted. "I was thinking that maybe we could go for dinner?"

"If you mean down to the dining room," he added, chuckling, "I think that's doable."

"And, if you'll take Hoppers back home, then maybe I have time for a shower."

"Why don't you do that." He walked over, picked up Hoppers, who at this point in time was quite comfortable in Quinton's arms and absolutely not interested in moving.

She smiled. "It's quite something to see him like this," she murmured.

"He's a beautiful animal inside and out. We kept him as one of our therapy animals," he said, with an eye roll. "We are collecting quite a crew of therapy animals."

"I guess the decision becomes, when is it a therapy animal and when is it just good therapy for you to save an animal?"

Surprised at her insight and yet realizing how true it was, he nodded immediately. "Absolutely. These guys are special to me."

"I think they're special to everybody who sees them," she said gently. "Not just to you."

"I hope so. There is a lot to be said for having them around."

"This guy looks to be pretty special," she murmured.

"I think so, but then, you know, that's just me." He turned, walked to the door with Hoppers, and asked, "So, should I meet you back here in ten minutes?"

She considered it, looked down at yourself, and shook her head. "Fifteen. I'm not that fast right now."

"Fifteen it is. I'll see you then." And, with his armload, he turned, and he walked out. As soon as he stepped into the main hallway, he stopped. A group of people had gathered at the end of the hallway. They took one look at him, grinned, and then disappeared. He just stared at Dani. "Really?"

"Everybody hurts when one of us hurts," she admitted. "But it seems like things are much better."

"I think so. At least I hope so. Honestly, at this point, it's going to be a case of time will tell."

"That works for me." She cuddled Hoppers's head and ears for a moment, her fingers stroking the bunny's long silky ears. "This guy continuously amazes me. Does he ever stop growing?"

"I think he's stopped." Stan frowned. "But maybe not."

"Maybe not is right. And that's okay too. He gets to be who he is, and we're not going to knock him for that."

"Glad to hear that." Stan smiled. "Now I'm going to take him back to his place."

"You do that, and we'll see you at dinnertime." She stopped to stare at him, then looked back at the door behind him. "Is she coming?"

He nodded. "She is."

"Good," Dani said. "I keep hoping that she'll remember who's important in all this."

"I think she's working on it right now," he replied. "She did have some interesting insights and was wondering what she should do in many areas. So I think it's just a matter of time."

"And I'd be very grateful if that were the case. She's a really good person," Dani noted, "and I'm really happy for you. I thought maybe it would have happened last time. Yet it didn't seem to go anywhere."

"No." He shook his head. "It didn't, and that's okay too."

She nodded, walked closer, reached up, and kissed him gently on the cheek. "All good things come to those who wait."

He smirked. "Well, that hasn't exactly been my experience."

"But it's a whole new dawn out there." She chuckled. "Don't knock it before you try it." And, with that, she turned and left, heading toward the dining room herself.

As he walked slowly, carrying Hoppers back to his hutch, Stan wondered at the sudden shift in his life. He could hope that this was for real. But he also knew that, even if it wasn't, he'd learned a lot about the people around him. And the fact that, to them, he really was somebody they cared about.

And he liked hearing that; he liked knowing that he was appreciated for who he was. Not something he particularly had ever needed to feel or had even thought to feel here. But it truly was a boon. And one he was grateful to have.

He hadn't realized how much his own sense of self, his own sense of self-esteem, had taken a hit by Quinton's words. And it wasn't fair—just as she had given away her power and her positivity to the injury that she currently found herself dealing with yet again, thinking her rehab days were all over with and would never come back again.

Stan had done the same thing with her, giving away that hope of a relationship with her all those years ago. Not something he was terribly proud of, and nothing he really wanted to repeat. But it was a learning process for both of them, and he wasn't at all upset about having learned one very important lesson. He needed to tell her how he felt, and hear the same from her. They should all share these pleasant, encouraging words with each other more often.

And now he could hope that together they could get stronger, faster, and better after this. They just needed time. And that was something he was fully prepared to give her, as much time as she needed.

Chapter 11

QUINTON MOVED THROUGH the next few days with a smile on her face and a hum in her heart. Even Shane's workouts couldn't have done anything to destroy it. Although it seemed like Shane was trying. And yet that wasn't fair; it appeared that so much more went on in the fitness world that she had no way to get ahead of it. She even said that to Shane.

He looked at her and smiled. "That's actually a good way to look at it," he noted, "but I promise we will get ahead of it, and you will have this long list of things that you need to do on a daily basis and some on a weekly basis."

She stared at him. "Seriously?"

He nodded. "If you're not here for months with us," he explained, "it's going to take a while to retrain those muscles to do what they need to do properly."

"Wow." She scrubbed her face with her hands. It was hard to explain the sinking feeling in her stomach and that sag in her mood. "I was thinking that this wouldn't be something I had to maintain."

"You must maintain it for life," he stated. He crouched down in front of her.

She sat with her legs pulled to her chest, staring at him.

"It didn't take you five minutes to get into this misalignment," he explained, "and it won't take you five minutes to get out of it. Eventually you'll get to the point where it'll be incorporated into a biweekly stretch/yoga-type routine," he explained, "but you're not there yet. So expect six months of this routine at home." And, with that, he smiled. "Now it's almost dinnertime. I presume you're meeting up with Stan?"

"Actually I don't know. I haven't heard from him all day. He told me earlier how he would be late with surgeries." She looked down at her watch and nodded. "I thought maybe I'd stop in and see my brother."

"Good enough," Shane agreed. "That might shift his mood too." She looked at him in surprise. He shrugged. "Seems to be going through something these days." And, with that, he walked out.

Slowly Quinton pulled herself up into her wheelchair, checking on her stump. It had taken some abuse lately. Just a little bit of blistering and scrapes. She'd banged it up a couple times, and she definitely saw some bruising too.

Tired, but an inner fatigue, after having had a decent session with Shane, Quinton moved out of the workout room into the hallway, reoriented herself and turned in the direction of her brother's room. When she got to his room, she knocked. When she got no answer, she knocked again.

He called out, "Fine, come in."

She turned the knob and awkwardly pushed open the door enough to get her wheelchair inside. Once there, she saw him lying in bed, a blanket atop him. Immediately she felt fear taking over. "Bad day?" she asked.

He rolled his head toward her, nodded, and replied, "Bad life."

"Yeah, I had a few days like that too," she agreed, settling back in her wheelchair. "Stan's doing surgeries late tonight. How about dinner?"

"Meaning that I'm not your first choice, but you don't want to go alone, so I'm better than nothing?"

"Is that really what you think?" she asked, frowning.

"Maybe. It kind of goes along with the way you just presented the invitation."

"I didn't mean it that way," she replied, wondering at her poor choice of words. "I just meant that I have an opening in my schedule that I'm not filling with Stan at the moment, and I would like to spend it with you."

He sighed. "That's marginally better."

Such a bitter note was in his tone. "What's going on?" she asked.

"Nothing."

But she noted his jaw locking and a tick in the corner of his mouth. "So …?"

Once again he rolled his head toward her. "Remember that friend of mine?"

She shook her head. "Nope, don't think you've mentioned anybody."

"Well, my long-term friend, put it that way."

"Ah, Helena?"

He nodded. "She got married this weekend."

"Oh, how nice for her," she replied, with real joy. "You always did like her."

"Yeah, that's the problem."

She stopped, and it took her a few minutes. Then she winced. "Are you saying you more than liked her?"

"I don't know," he admitted. "She's been on my mind a lot."

"Maybe she's been on your mind because you knew the wedding was coming up and your paths were diverging."

"Sure." He gave her a hand wave. "Whatever that means."

"It doesn't necessarily mean that you wanted more than a friendship from her. Because, if you had, why wouldn't you have done something about it in the previous … what? I don't know. Ten years?"

"Because I thought there was time," he stated. "I know she wouldn't be a fan of me in the military. And I was waiting for maybe a time when I wouldn't stay in the military."

"Well, depending on how she felt about you being in the service," she replied, "she probably wouldn't hang around and wait for you."

"Maybe not," he said. "I just kind of feel like it was a lost opportunity."

Quinton knew how that felt. She nodded. "Which is why I'm giving Stan and me a chance."

"Seriously?" he asked.

She nodded. "At least I'm trying."

"And what about him? Is he trying?"

"Yes." She studied her brother carefully. "I get that you are in a rather odd mood, and, if you don't want to come that's fine. I am going to have a shower first, but, after that, I just thought it might be nice to have some family time. I won't be here for too much longer."

"Right, because you have a life. You get to leave this prison and to go on to whatever it is that you want to go on to."

Surprised at the sarcastic and hurtful tone in his voice, she pushed her wheelchair backward. "I don't really need to sit here and to hear this," she stated. "My own mood is rather fragile at the moment, so, in self-preservation mode,

I'm going to rescind the dinner invitation, and I'll have that shower. Maybe at the end of that I'll feel better than after listening to you," she added. "It's really time for you to pull yourself up by the bootstraps and to stop playing the *poor me* card as much as you are. You have the gift of being here. I suggest you start appreciating that."

"Like you did, *huh?*' he asked, with a snort. "You think I haven't heard all the rumors about how you weren't going to stay and how everybody had to coax you to stay?" He rolled his eyes. "Like, give me a break."

She felt the hurt magnifying inside. *Was there ever anybody who could hurt you as much as somebody you cared about?* She didn't think so, just like she'd hurt Stan so much. "I get that you're having a rough time," she said, "but that's really no excuse for hitting out and trying to hurt me at the same time."

"Is that what I'm doing?" he asked, brooding still, as he turned and faced the window. "Just seems like I'm lashing out at everybody, doesn't matter who, so you're nobody special."

"And there we go again. Got it. I'll talk to you later." And she pushed his door open and rolled through the doorway, making an awkward job of it because, of course, she still wasn't used to the wheelchair mobility thing. Now her hands were shaking. She moved through the hallway toward her own room. Her bed was looking awfully inviting. But she was still hot and sticky. She made it to the shower, and, by the time she was clean and redressed, she was exhausted. She curled up on the bed, feeling the hot tears in the back of her eyes.

Ryatt had always been a decent person, never one to really throw out hurtful comments. She wasn't sure how much

Helena's wedding had to do with this—or was it more about how much he was probably looking back down the long tunnel of his life's choices and wondering where he'd gone wrong?

Quinton had a few of those tunnels herself. And it was foolish to feel so emotionally overwrought about her brother, who was going through a bad period. He was throwing darts, and she was accepting them. That's where the problem came in. She needed to just pull the darts free and get rid of them.

Instead it was just a little more than she could handle right now. She closed her eyes and curled up with a blanket tucked up to her shoulders. When she woke again, she wasn't surprised to realize that dinner was almost over. Knowing that she would wake up hungry and be *hangry* through the night and ugly in the morning, she pulled herself into her wheelchair and slowly made her way to the dining area. As she stepped in line, Stan was ahead of her, visibly tired and worn out. "Stan?"

He turned, looked at her. "Hey," he said, walking closer. And then he frowned, as he noted she was getting in line. "Haven't you had dinner?"

She shook her head. In a low voice she said, "I had words with my brother, went back to my room, and fell asleep." He studied her gaze, and she realized some tear stains probably remained that she hadn't even bothered to wipe free.

He reached up a gentle hand, stroked her cheek, and said, "Well, that's good timing then for me." He smiled. "Would you do me the honor of eating with me tonight?"

She beamed. "Thank you. I could use that tonight."

Dennis was nearby, watching the two of them. "Glad to see you showed up," he said, shaking the serving spoon at

Quinton. "You don't want to make me come down to your room and chase you out."

She smiled. "You would have woken me up, if you had."

Immediately he nodded. "Yep, some days are like that, aren't they?"

"Today's definitely one of them." She wandered closer to the buffet line. "What's for dinner?"

"Roast beef is what I've got the most of," he replied, "but we've got some fish left here too."

She wasn't sure what kind of fish but it was battered. *Yum.* She hesitated.

Dennis quickly offered, "How about a little of both?"

She smiled. "That sounds great."

He loaded her plate with the two meat dishes and lots of vegetables and handed it over to her. With Stan at her side and doing a couple more trips, they finally made their way out onto the deck.

"At least by eating at this hour," she noted, "it's cooled down."

He nodded. "I'll go grab dessert because Dennis will be cleaning up soon. Do you want something?"

She smiled. "Yes, get me whatever you are getting, and would you mind getting me some water too, please?" He nodded and disappeared. She took their plates off the trays, stacked the trays on another table, and sniffed the food on her plate. She was really hungry now.

She almost wished that she'd asked for twice as much meat. But maybe Dennis wouldn't close up quite so fast. She took a bite of the roast beef, without waiting for Stan, and then moaned. "Oh, God, that's good," she whispered.

Stan returned moments later with two large pieces of chocolate cake and water bottles for both of them.

She pointed at her plate. "The roast beef's really, really good. I wish I'd gotten more." He nodded, looked at his plate, and added, "I'm really hungry too. Hang on." He disappeared again.

She didn't even bother twisting around to watch whatever Stan was doing, as she took several more bites. When he returned, he brought her a plate with just roast beef and gravy on it. She stared at it, smiling.

"No point in waiting until after Dennis has already put it all away. We can share what we want off this plate."

She laughed. "No matter how hungry I think I am, or how delicious this roast is, I still don't think I can eat everything on both plates."

"Well, good for you," he said, "because I'm going to give it the old college try." And he did. They both tucked into their meals. After the first pangs of hunger had abated, Stan asked, "Is your brother okay?"

"Another bad patch," she replied, with a shrug. "He's shooting darts at me."

"Ah, dang. When those suckers find a home, they hurt."

"They sure do," she admitted. "But I can see that, at the moment, he's just looking at his life choices—wondering if he should have changed a few of them."

"I think we all do that at times," Stan agreed. "I was in my third year of vet school when I wondered what I was doing there."

She stared at him in shock. "No way."

He nodded. "I just got back an exam, where I hadn't done anywhere near as well as I thought I should have, and the professor had written a caustic comment on the top of the first page. It will never leave me, but he said, *And you're one of the ones we let in? ... Why?*"

"Ouch." Quinton stared at him in shock. "I hope you got him in trouble for that."

Stan laughed. "No, he was right. I was one of the ones allowed into the veterinary school. And I hadn't done as well on that exam as I thought I should have. And maybe his word of warning was a wake-up call. I don't know, but I certainly spent some time doing some soul-searching and trying to figure out just why I was where I was."

"And what was the answer?" she asked curiously, as she tackled her vegetables.

"The answer was simple. I always wanted to work with animals," he stated. "I could have been an MD, a surgeon, but that didn't appeal. Working with people as patients, you must have a special ability to deal with them, and I didn't think I had it."

She slowly put down her fork, reached across, grabbed his hand, and squeezed. "You're wrong. You're very good with people."

Surprised, he looked at her fingers. He squeezed her hand gently, then forked up a bite of meat into his mouth, chewing while considering her words. After he had thoroughly chewed and swallowed that bite, he said, "Thank you. It's not something I often get told."

"And that's one of the things that's the problem with life," she noted, "is I think we forget to tell people anything."

"No, you're right," he agreed. "We tell them the bad things, but we rarely tell them the good things."

"And I'm just as guilty," she admitted. "As I'm sitting here thinking about it," she realized, "I feel like I haven't said anything nice to my brother in a very long time." Stan kept eating, while she thought about it. She sighed. "And maybe, ... maybe the darts he's throwing are because he feels unloved."

"I think everybody feels that way too much of the time, and, when they feel unloved—that they aren't worthy of love, which causes them pain and hurt—they lash out."

"I did tell him to stop lashing out at me," she added, with a half smile. "So my self-confidence showed up. Maybe I should have told him also that, regardless, I love him anyway."

"There's nothing stopping you from doing that," Stan told her gently. "You're here for a while longer. Make sure that finding a way to mend some bridges with him is part of this."

"Wouldn't that be nice." She looked over at the extra plate with the roast beef and back at him.

He grinned. "There's lots on that one plate. Have as much as you want."

They each took one slice, and still one more remained. He cut it in half and divvied it up between their plates. When he was done, she scooped the last of the gravy off the plate onto hers.

"I really do like the food here," she murmured.

"I do too," he agreed, "and I'm blessed. I get it all the time."

She smiled. "You are, indeed, blessed." By the time she had finished the roast beef, she was stuffed. She pushed away the plates and said, "My gosh, that was a lot of food."

He nodded. "And we don't have to eat the cake right now," he suggested. "We can just sit here and relax for a while."

"I hear you. That sounds like a good idea too." She smiled and looked across at him. "I'm really glad you were late today. Hopefully it wasn't a terrible day."

Stan smiled, patted her hand gently, but didn't say anything.

But Quinton was perceptive enough to know that something was up. "I gather it was terrible."

He nodded. "A surgery didn't go well, and I had to put down an animal. It's never a good day when you have to start off your morning killing something."

She winced. "No." She stared off at the hills. "You may have wanted to work with animals, but you need to be commended because I can't imagine that would always be easy. And that's what makes you such a good veterinarian, your compassion and humanity."

"It's also," he stated, with a half smile as he looked at her, "why I hurt a little more easily than I'd like to." He knew she would immediately feel guilty, due to their recent breakup, so he added in a stronger voice, "And maybe, maybe your brother's like that too."

"He's always been a softy. He's always been an animal lover. And I know that he's very easily affected by people who've walked out of his life." And then she stopped. She sat here, stared at him, and said, "You know what? That's why this friend of his who just got married is affecting him so badly."

Stan looked at her, and she quickly explained. He nodded. "Ah, so he was wondering if maybe she could have been somebody better than a friend?"

"I think it was always an idea in the back of his mind, but, if it wasn't more than just an idea to consider, I think he would have done something about it. Yet the fact that she's married now, I think in a way, is bothering him the most because he may be afraid that that will end their friendship."

"It may not end it," Stan said, "but it will definitely change it. Nothing like a marriage to bring in another person who may or may not gel with a group of friends. I've seen a lot of couples break up—or couples who break up with friends—because a new person joined the group and wasn't necessarily a great match."

She smiled. "It's funny how to think that a union—supposedly to make us better—ends up separating us from all of what we know sometimes." She nodded. "I've had friends like that. And when they chose somebody we were just completely shocked by, they just smiled and said it was their choice. One friend in particular, she walked away from us, and that was that," she explained. "We were all quite upset about it. I haven't thought about her in a long time." Quinton stared off in the distance. "It's … Again it's those glances down the tunnels of our past."

Stan smiled, pushed the chocolate cake toward her, and said, "And that's making us gloomy, so let's have something sweet to lighten it up."

She laughed when she looked down at the size of the piece. "Are you sure you didn't squish two pieces together in order to make it look just like one?"

"Nope, sure didn't, but they were the two biggest I could find." He grinned, as Quinton picked up her fork and tackled it. He was surprised at the amount of food she could put away. But a healing body required sustenance. And definitely sustenance was required when she was back here doing as much of the rehab work that she was doing. "How's your progress?"

She nodded. "Well, it's going. Unfortunately Shane says I'll be still at it for six more months, likely six months," she corrected, "doing these kinds of exercises and stretches every day, before I can get into a biweekly routine."

"I don't think that sounds all that bad," he noted. "I've seen patients here for longer than that. So it really does sound like you're on track."

"Maybe … but somehow it doesn't seem like it. It feels almost like a life sentence."

He looked at her and smiled. "I don't think a *life sentence* is quite the right phrase. How about a *gift of life* instead?"

Chapter 12

S TAN'S WORDS ONCE again hung around in Quinton's head for the next few days. Stan was busy in town, had a conference, and so she didn't have dinner with him for the next couple days. By the time Friday rolled around, she found herself missing him something terrible. And something was good and solid about missing him. *I should be missing him*, she realized. Stan should be somebody she didn't want to be apart from. She just didn't realize how much she would miss him. She also missed her brother, and yet he was right here, just distant, and she had to give him his space.

She realized that she had some mending there to do too. Late Friday afternoon, after one of her appointments had been canceled, she headed to her brother's room, not at all sure if he was even there. But knowing her time at Hathaway House was starting to run out, she knocked on his door.

He called out in a much stronger voice, "Come in."

She opened the door, stuck her head in, and asked, "Hey, are you up for a visitor?"

He smiled, nodded, and replied, "Yeah, we probably should."

"Probably should what?"

"Talk," he said. "I presume you're leaving soon."

She winced. "I think I have another week."

"A week can go by just like that," he noted, with a snap of his fingers. "I've been here almost seven weeks now."

"Any improvement?"

"You know what? For the first time today, I'm not feeling like rubber on pavement spread so thin that it can't cover the road," he murmured. "I'm tired, but it's not an exhausted tired. It's more of a feel-good accomplishment."

She smiled as she stared at him. "All of that sounds like an improvement."

"It is. And I owe you an apology," he said abruptly.

And again she stared at him in surprise. What had happened to her brother?

"I was a fool, and I was hurt and was hitting out at you."

"And why were you hurt?"

His grin turned lopsided. "I was wallowing, wallowing in the what-ifs. But they weren't what-ifs with any kind of sincerity. They were just what-ifs of life."

"Helena?"

He nodded. "And I'm slowly adapting to the idea that I'm going to lose her."

"Do you have to?"

"No, not necessarily," he replied, "but our paths diverged a long time ago. It was me, hanging on to the tentacles of what I thought was an enduring friendship, but I don't think it was. I think I liked her for who she was in my mind but not necessarily for who she really was."

"Were you invited to the wedding?"

"Nope. I saw it on social media. That was kind of another blow."

"So maybe she wasn't so much of a friend as an acquaintance?"

"I guess," he said, "but it was the one that I always kept

in the back of my mind that, you know, should my circumstances change then ..."

"I'm sorry," Quinton said. "You always did take abandonment hard."

He winced. "Yeah, don't worry. I had that out with a shrink session too."

"Good, sounds like it was a very necessary talk."

"Well, it was a productive one," he noted. "I was feeling pretty rough for a couple days, but I have to admit. Today I feel like I'm going to live."

"Yeah, some of that emotional stuff is by far the worst," she shared.

"One of the things that came out," he shared carefully, "was the fact that some people in my life kept coming back and that—even though at times I felt like I had been isolated and abandoned—in fact, I hadn't been."

"Good," she stated encouragingly. "We need some stability in our world, some routine, some faces that are the same over and over again."

He nodded. "Have you been to dinner yet?"

"Not yet, it's actually early."

He nodded. "It is, indeed. I just wondered if Stan was going to be there for dinner."

"No, he's in town."

"Ah, so sorry," he teased in a mocking voice.

Not sure how great her brother was if this was the mood he was in, still she laughed. "I guess the heart grows fonder the more we're apart."

"Is it serious?"

Her lips tilted. "Yes, I think so, although I haven't told him that."

Ryatt stared at her, shaking his head. "Well, from somebody who hung on to something that wasn't serious at all, but in my mind I thought maybe could be, do him a favor and tell him."

"We haven't come to that kind of a talk yet," she said.

"No, but you should also be aware whether it's happening or not. Lord knows, you guys spend enough time together."

"We actually don't," she stated. "We spend a couple evenings out on the deck, and we've had a few breakfasts or lunches together, and he pops in when he can, but he's had a really crazy-busy couple weeks."

"It's his own business too, isn't it?"

"Yes, it is. And, of course, a lot of animals and staff depend on him."

"No, I get that," Ryatt added. "I still think it's important for you to make it clear to him where he stands."

And she thought about his words for a while and then nodded. "Yeah, you're probably right. I need to do something in that direction. I just haven't yet."

He smiled. "You do have a week still," he reminded her, "but I would certainly not want to see you leaving here with him in limbo."

"I wouldn't do that," she automatically said. But, of course, she had been. She hadn't given him an update on how she felt at all. But then it seemed like time was going by so quickly that she didn't even know quite what to do. She looked at her brother. "What about you? You settling in better?"

"I am now," he said, looking over at her. "It's going to take a bit, but I think I've turned a corner. And I mean that with all honesty."

"I'm delighted to hear that." She nodded, then pointed

at the door. "Anyway I'm going to head back and maybe do some journaling before dinner."

"You didn't ask who it was who was the constant in my life," he stated.

She stopped, as she headed to the door. "No, I didn't. Why?"

"Don't you want to know?"

She shrugged. "You'll tell me if you want to."

He laughed. "You're the only constant," he said, with a smile. "You're the only one who—even when I'm an absolute ass to you—keeps coming back. And I understand what that is, and it's called love. I just wanted to let you know that I appreciate it. From the bottom of my heart. I know I haven't been very good to anybody around here and especially not to you lately," he added, "but I'm determined to improve on that."

She felt the tears choking the back of her throat. "Thank you." And then she remembered what she had talked about with Stan, and she added, "You really are one of the best brothers I could have. You've hit a bad patch, a couple of them, same as me, but that doesn't mean you're rotten all the way through. We had a lot of good times before, and we'll have a lot of good times together in the future too. The constant between us is the fact that it's us," she said, with a smile. "Let's not keep complaining about us. Let's just rebuild stronger and better because, bro, I love you."

And, with that, she lifted a hand and pushed her way out of the room. Her heart full and her soul beaming, she headed to her room, hopeful for whatever came next.

STAN WALKED THROUGH the upstairs patient lounge. He had an unusual pet for them to visit with. He had a ferret in his arms. It was on a leash and a harness but wasn't feeling 100 percent up to snuff, having just recovered from surgery, gone home, and was now back again for some therapy. He was certainly friendly enough but he was tired and didn't walk well.

Stan was carrying him, holding him up on his shoulder so he could see the sights. And a happy camper he was. As Stan stopped to visit with several people in a group by a foosball table, one of them noticed the animal on his shoulder and chortled.

"Oh, now look at that. My granny had one of those as a pet."

"Yeah?" Stan said. "They're quite the lively characters. I wouldn't mind having one myself."

"Hey, you could have any kind of pet you wanted," the guy said. "At least you get a lot of exposure to them here."

"I do," he agreed, with a smile. The guy reached up, and Stan obligingly bent over a little bit more. The ferret, whose name was Fuzz, jumped onto the other man's shoulder, both startling and delighting them. "Well, would you look at that," Stan said.

Almost immediately his group of friends gathered around. Loving caresses were exchanged as the ferret soaked, basked even, in the sweet attention he was getting.

Stan chuckled. "I always think these guys don't really care about people, and then I bring them around, and look at that? They become needy almost instantly."

"Everybody's needy," one of the guys replied. "We all need love and attention, even little ones like this."

"Isn't that the truth," Stan said, with feeling.

"I hear you've got quite a mighty fine-looking woman," one of them noted.

And that let Stan know that the gossip machine was working just fine here as always. "She is, indeed," he replied.

As soon as the ferret appeared to be getting a little bit bored with this set of company, Stan told him, "Come on, Fuzz. Let's move on." And Fuzz obligingly jumped onto his shoulder, and they carried on down to the next group. By the time Stan had worked his way up to the hallway on the other side and knocked on a couple doors to see if anybody wanted to visit, he found himself at Ryatt's door. Stan hesitated and then shrugged, knocked on the door anyway.

When the call came to come in, he pushed open the door, stuck his head around, and asked, "Did you want to see this guy?"

Ryatt looked at him in surprise and then saw Fuzz on his shoulder. "Wow, you really do have assorted animals down there, don't you?"

"Yeah, sure do," he agreed. "This guy had surgery and went home, had rehab, didn't do so well, so he's back here for some more intensive rehab."

Ryatt noted, "Oh, sounds like my sister." When Stan raised his eyebrows, Ryatt shrugged. "She's back again, isn't she?"

"Yeah, hopefully she doesn't have to stay very long though, just like this guy."

"Is he not here for long?" he asked.

"Nope, not for long, a couple days. We're giving him quite a run-through and a set of testing, so we can set up a home program for him."

"You set up rehab programs for animals?" Ryatt looked as if the entire concept had struck him dumb.

"Well, it makes sense, doesn't it?" Stan asked, studying Ryatt. "When you think about it, somebody's got to."

"I just hadn't considered it," he admitted, "and yet it makes total sense. I would have never thought of it, so I'm glad somebody else did, especially for this guy if it makes him feel better."

"That's what it's all about, making them feel better," Stan noted. "Come on. Let's go, Fuzz."

"*Fuzz.*" Ryatt chuckled. "You had to give him a name like that, *huh?*"

"I didn't give him the name," Stan explained. "He earned the moniker all on his own. Apparently he sticks to things like fuzz."

"Interesting," he murmured. "I heard they were quite the collectors."

"Precisely, things stick to him like fuzz, put it that way," Stan added, with a grin.

As he went to leave, Ryatt called out, "How serious is it with my sister?"

Stan wasn't offended. He stopped, looked at her brother, and told him truthfully, "I hope it's serious, but it's early days yet."

Ryatt nodded. "I appreciate the fact that she has you. I know she's had a rough time of it."

"I think at some point in time we all have rough patches," Stan admitted. "Those of us who are lucky have a friend or family member who can help us see beyond the tunnel of our pain."

Again Ryatt looked at him in surprise. "That's very true—for those of us who are lucky enough."

"And it doesn't always happen the way we think it does," Stan added. "Some people think that that kind of help is just there automatically, and it's often not. Sometimes it's something that you have to work at. Sometimes it's something that you really have to take another look at the people around you and realize that they really are there for you, even if you didn't think so."

Ryatt nodded again. "No, I hear you. Just not really what I expected from the veterinarian here."

"Everybody here is a philosopher, and everybody here's a shrink," Stan said, laughing. "Best not to ask any of us questions like that." And, with that, and a wave of his hand, he stepped out.

He had no idea if he'd passed muster with Quinton's brother or not. After all, he was her family. And Stan wanted to make a good impression, but he'd known Quinton a little bit beforehand, but not as much as now. And it remained to be seen whether Quinton passed judgment on Stan or not.

And it really wasn't for Ryatt to do either, but that didn't stop any family member from stepping up and saying something. Stan hoped he'd get a decent rating from Ryatt for today's visit, but, if not, well, Stan would deal with it the same as he dealt with everything else in life. Stan hadn't been joking when he had said to his staff at the clinic that he wasn't any good with this relationship stuff because he was really a plain-talking kind of guy.

He called a spade a spade, and, if it wasn't a spade, and he didn't know what it was, then he would say that he didn't know what it was. He wasn't one to bluff and to lie and to find some kind of an answer that might make him look or sound better. Wasn't his style. Then again that's probably why he hadn't done all that well in that whole relationship cycle in school. Most people succeeded with some suave polish that Stan couldn't even hope to imitate, so he hadn't bothered. He'd always figured that, if he had to imitate something, that it wouldn't come from the heart anyway.

Not sure it had done him any good to follow that path, but it's what he'd done. Meanwhile he had yet to be married. Still he could easily see himself spending his life with Quinton, and he hoped she would come to that decision too. He wasn't all that old, although he knew that, if he looked in the mirror, it seemed like he was older.

Some days in the clinic were just that much harder than others too, which made him age as well. Some days were just deadly. Particularly days when he lost lives. Anytime something was heartbreakingly wrong, it affected everybody. But, like anything, you had to pick up your feet and get on with life. The next day would only be as good as you could make it. Other than that, you would just wallow, and life never, ever changed.

For Stan, that wasn't acceptable. He was always looking to improve, always looking to change and to do something more. He just hoped that Quinton was on the same page. Because, if she wasn't, it would be one heartbreak that he might not recover from.

Chapter 13

I T TOOK QUINTON a few more days of getting through Shane's heavy workouts to understand what she was doing wrong all the time and how to fix it. Good thing she'd taken Stan's advice to take three months leave. But slowly and steadily Quinton was pulling her body back into alignment, and everything was starting to feel a whole lot more in sync. It was almost as if she'd been disjointed before, and things were slipping out of place, but, with Shane's careful training, she felt more normal again.

When she tried to explain that to him, he just nodded. "When you're out of alignment, everything goes out of whack. It's so important to get that, to have everything just staying where it needs to be. And don't feel bad that it happened," he told her. "It happens to the best of us, including me. It's very easy to forget what you're doing and to let things slide. In your case, letting things slide is going to be a bigger issue because of the existing physical issues you have," he noted. "It's not something that you'll have to do every day for the rest of your life, but it is something that you'll have to keep an eye on every day."

She nodded. "That's fine. I might need a reminder of that every once in a while."

"I agree. Set yourself a reminder, set yourself a wellness check, send yourself to a spa for a day or two," he murmured. "Whatever it is you need to do, take time out and just reevaluate where your body's at and what it's doing, how it's feeling, then do what you need to do. There is no greater gift that you can give to yourself than the gift of health."

When he left at the end of that rehab session, she still sat here in the workout room, pondering his words. When she finally looked up, Stan stood there, with a smile on his face.

"You okay?" he asked.

She heard the worry in the back of his voice. "I'm fine. I think one of the things that always gets me when I'm here is that inherent wisdom that keeps coming out of everybody's mouth."

He burst out laughing. "Right? Hathaway House is the place for it," he murmured. "And sometimes they say the darndest things."

"You do too." She smiled and gave a wave of her hand. "I'm including you in this whole mess too."

"I don't know about that. I'm just the dumb klutz down in the basement with the animals. In the olden days I'd have been living in the barn with them."

She smiled. "In the olden days I probably would have been there with you," she murmured.

He smiled ever-so-gently. "Then there's no place I'd rather be."

She looked up at him and chuckled. "I presume it's dinnertime."

"Not yet, but we're getting there."

She nodded. "I need a shower. Today's physio session was a little rough."

"I think all the sessions with Shane are a little rough," he noted. "At least I keep hearing that from a lot of people."

"He knows what he's doing, and he asks a lot from us.

Yet it's never more than he would do himself, so you don't mind doing it. At the same time, when he's done, so are you."

Stan burst out laughing at that. "And that's probably a fair way to look at it." He gave her a wide smile. "So how about dinner in, what, an hour?"

She nodded, but then frowned and looked around. "You know something? I think I really need to go to the pool."

"Okay, so dinner in an hour and a half?" he asked.

She smiled. "Are you off work now?" He nodded. "So join me," she said. "Let's meet at the pool." He pondered it, and she added, "There's no better way to release that stress from a long day."

"It has been a long day," he muttered. "And you're right. I could really use it. Fine, I'll … I'll meet you down there in a little bit."

"Good. We don't want to leave too late, but we also can't intrude on somebody having a rehab session going on right now."

"Right," he murmured. "I can also take a look as I go down."

"Sure, why not, and you can always send me a message." And then she added, "Don't worry about it. I'm going to go regardless. If nothing else, I can sit in the hot tub and relax that way."

"Okay. I'll meet you there in ten. I have to go find my suit."

She smiled as he took off. It would be wonderful to live someplace where she could meet in ten minutes and be at the hot tub and the pool. She might have to seriously rethink her living accommodations. Like, wow, what a place to work and to live. She knew a lot of the staff lived and worked here.

And a lot of them liked it, while some preferred to be in town, where they had other family members and spouses.

But for Quinton? She would enjoy this scenario while she had it available. She changed, not quickly, but she managed to get into her suit, back into the wheelchair, and, with every push of the wheelchair, she felt herself draining further and further.

She'd forgotten to ask Shane again about her prosthetic. Whether they could try it now. She hadn't been using it the entire time she had been here, so all the sores could heal up. She was rather desperate to get back on two legs again. She had such a different feeling when she stood upright, like homo sapiens were meant to. And yet she hadn't pushed it. She pondered that, as she shifted toward the pool area.

As she got closer, she saw her brother there with Shane, working out. She thought if she could get him to spare a moment, she could ask him now. But she didn't want to interrupt her brother's session. These sessions were too important. When she found Shane staring at her, she shrugged. "Are we allowed?"

He nodded. "We're almost done." He checked his watch. "I'm surprised to see you, since you were pretty tired."

"I'm still tired," she admitted, "but I'm here."

"Good," he murmured.

"I would like to ask," she added, "any chance we can start working on the prosthetic again?"

"We need to see if it still fits," he stated. "You may have to get a new one."

She winced at that because that could take a long time. "You think it's not been fitted properly?"

"Well, it depends," he noted, with a chuckle. "You haven't been standing properly, so you haven't been using it properly, and, therefore, I don't know if it works well for you now or not."

She groaned. "We're back to that again, huh?"

"We sure are," he said, with a smile. "It all comes back to posture. Everything comes back to alignment."

She nodded and managed to get herself close enough to the pool and locked the wheels. Then on one leg, grabbing the ladder, she hobbled over closer and fell into the pool itself. When she surfaced, her brother splashed her in the face. She chuckled. "What was that for?" she asked, splashing him back.

"Just felt like it," he replied, with a chuckle. "Haven't been able to splash you like that in a long time."

"Isn't that the truth," she said in delight. "As I recall, I probably owe you more than a few." And she proceeded to grab his head and try to dunk him. By the time he had retaliated, and she'd retaliated a couple times herself, they were both exhausted.

She pulled herself up to the side of the pool and just sat on the edge there. Shane had a big grin on his face. "We're still siblings," she confirmed.

He nodded. "And that kind of play—when it's all done in good fun," he stated, "is huge. Just think about all the muscles and the energy you expended."

"Yeah, I'm thinking about it," she noted, groaning. "I'm exhausted now. And the thought of getting back to my room is even more exhausting." Now Stan had shown up too. She smiled up at him. "Hopefully you didn't see that childish display of affection," she said, with a big grin.

"Absolutely I didn't." But his grin was wide enough to tell her that he certainly had.

She sighed. "Not exactly the kind of impression I'd want to make."

"Hey, you're well past the point of making an impression with anybody here," her brother teased, as he heaved up onto the pool edge beside her. He looked over at her and added, "It's good to see you again, kiddo."

"Ditto," she murmured. And it really was good to see him—especially seeing him like this, seeing him feeling a whole lot better, a little bit more like she'd expected to see him. She groaned as she looked down at the water. "I don't know what Shane's got you doing in here," she said, "but he beats me up when it's my turn."

At that, Shane protested.

She shook her head. "No, no, I'm not letting you off the hook on that one," she argued. "You know perfectly well that I'm right about that." And that started another session of joking and splashing water on Shane. This time her brother was on her side.

Finally Shane gave up the fight. "That's it. You guys are picking on me, so I'm leaving."

She smiled, as he headed off. "As long as there are no hard feelings." He lifted a hand amid his laughter. And she realized it was all good. She looked over at her brother. "I don't know about you, but I'm pretty tired now."

He nodded, obviously short on breath, and said, "Ditto, but I'm going to leave you to your lover boy. I'll head up, get a shower, and, if I'm lucky, I'll still have energy to grab some food." He shook his head. "I'm not sure right now that I can do that."

Stan suggested, "Contact Dennis if you need food delivered to your room."

At that comment, her brother looked at him and said, "I

suppose that's always an option, isn't it?"

"It is," Stan confirmed. "You don't always have to be the tough guy. There are some days when just getting out of bed is more than any of us can handle."

Ryatt looked at Stan and asked, "You too?"

"Yeah, me too," he admitted. "There are good days. There are bad days, and then there are all the rest in between that vary across the scale. And sometimes on some of those days it just isn't worth moving."

"Yeah, I get that part." Ryatt pulled himself up into his wheelchair, lifted a hand, and slowly pushed himself toward the elevator.

Quinton frowned, worried about him.

But Stan was here at her side, murmuring, "He's fine."

She winced. "It's that obvious?"

"You love him. You care for him We can't expect anything less."

"I don't know," she murmured. "Sometimes I think I shouldn't have brought him here."

"It would have been a different story if you hadn't come at the same time," he noted. "But the fact of the matter is, I think it's been good for you, good for both of you."

She looked over at him. "You can't fix everything. You know that, right?"

"No, I know that," he said. "I'm just going to fix everything within my capability to fix." And, with that, he looked at her and added, "Now it's my turn to get in the water. At least all the children have left for the day." And he waggled his eyebrows at her and jumped in.

Unfortunately she didn't have any energy to go in and splash Stan, like she'd done her brother. She'd certainly worn herself out earlier, and yet it felt good—like life again, enlivening, like she wasn't as much of an invalid as she had worried that she was. And maybe that's what it was all about, just that mind-set.

By the time the dinner bell came, she looked at Stan and asked him, "What are the chances of getting anybody to deliver food down here?"

He stared at her, nodding. "You know what? It's probably not a bad idea, but nobody has to deliver it. I'll go grab us some stuff. What do you want?" And he hopped up, grabbed a towel, and dried himself off.

"Anything," she said, "seriously, anything. I feel bad for asking." He stopped and glared at her. She threw up her hands. "I know. I know. I'm the broken one right now."

"You're not broken," he stated firmly. "You're the one fixing yourself."

"How? I'm not even doing anything. It's all I can do to get outside in the fresh air on a regular basis."

He shook his head. "You're doing more for yourself and your future than most." And he took off.

She wondered if he was right. Everyone needed to move ahead at their own pace. She rarely brought up her own future because it felt like she had so much still to do.

Just so many things in life that people thought were a done deal, and then suddenly they weren't, and maybe that's what this was all about too.

When Stan returned with two large plates, he set them on the outdoor table. "I'll be right back." Then he headed back up to get more. By the time he'd made two more trips, they had water and everything else they needed. She protested when he looked like he was ready to go up again. "Surely we don't need anything more. Now you'll make me feel really bad."

"Don't even go there," he replied. "He who can help should help."

At that, she frowned. "I'm sure that was a quote from somewhere, but I wouldn't know where."

He laughed. "Neither would I. It just sounded good. And I firmly believe that. We often get some of the patients up here who come down and help out in my office. The animals all need to know they're loved, and the humans all need to know that they're capable, and both just need acceptance. And that's the same for you. So stop making excuses and making things harder on yourself," he murmured. He looked around and raised one finger. "One more thing." And he disappeared.

Acceptance? Is that what this was all about? To make her feel like she was accepted just as she was right now? She hated the fact that insecurities were still rife within her. Mostly because she hadn't locked anything down. She hadn't told him anything—or at least not enough—and she hadn't given herself that same level of comfort. Which was kind of weird then because that kind of comfort was something that was so important.

And it didn't make a whole lot of sense to keep it from him. They needed to talk, and they needed to talk freely.

When he came back down, she looked up and smiled at him. "You are my constant in life."

Stan raised his eyebrows. "Wow. Where did that come from?"

"I needed to tell you something about how I feel. My brother told me to as well. In fact, he told me recently that I was his constant in his life. Funny, even my brother is wise in this place."

"Well then, here's to you and your brother," Stan replied, setting down his last item on the table.

"Is that wine?" she asked.

"It is, indeed. Dennis arranged it for us."

She smiled. "And what are we celebrating?"

"Well, I *hope* we're celebrating," he replied, "but I will take it on the chin like a man if we're not."

She frowned. "Sorry?"

"I'm really hoping," he said, "that we can clear the air once and for all."

She nodded, feeling her stomach churn, as she looked down at the food. "As long as it's all good news," she added. "I'm not sure I'm up for bad."

"You and me both," he agreed, with a smile. "You and me both." He popped the wine, poured them a glass, and then sat here and stared at her.

"Stan?" she asked uncertainly. "Are you okay?"

He shrugged. "Well, it's the most important time in my life," he stated.

Confused, uncertain, and now suddenly very worried, she reached for his hand. "I don't know what's going on," she murmured, "but I really don't want to do anything to jeopardize what we have."

"AND THE FIRST question is," Stan began, staring at Quinton, "what is it we have?"

And she realized it would be *that* kind of conversation. She whispered, "Something very precious, I hope."

He smiled. "Absolutely precious, but, at the same time, if it's not meant to be, I don't want to sit here, holding my breath for more."

"For more?" she asked. "You do know I'm damaged, right? And that I'm going to be a cripple for the rest of my life?"

He stared at her. "I don't know where you got that idea from, but you need to stop that now."

She glared at him. "What are you talking about?"

"Sometimes I wonder if you don't use your injuries," he explained carefully, as if feeling his way, "in order to keep people away."

"Well, keeping people away is usually a healthier idea," she declared, "than having people believe something that isn't there."

"And that's why we're having this conversation," he stated suddenly, "because I guess that's what I need to know."

"What do you need to know?" she asked, worried once again.

"Whether you care enough for us to keep going on this pathway," he said blatantly, "or whether you'll break it off because you're too afraid that what we have is real."

"Too afraid?" she repeated, staring at him. "Does it look like I'm afraid?"

"No, and I don't want to do this the wrong way, but it is very important to me that you understand that I'm not somebody who's only here for the good times. I'm somebody who's here for the long-term."

She smiled. "Anybody who doesn't understand that about you doesn't know you."

"And that's very true," he agreed. "So ..." He stopped, hesitated.

"You want to just spit it out?" she asked, laughing.

"When you were here as a patient last time," he confessed, "I really, really, *really* wanted to get to know you better. And, when you left, I felt like I'd missed out on an opportunity that I didn't … that I shouldn't have missed out on," he murmured. "And it was very hard on me. I … I was quite depressed for a very long time, never really understood what I was supposed to do about it, and then, all of a sudden, you were back again. Just distant. Formal. Business-like."

She smiled. "Well, sometimes good things come out of these injuries."

"A lot of good things come out of healing these injuries," he noted. "But they aren't always as obvious as we would like to think they are." He watched, sensing something in her own mood, as if she suddenly understood where he was going with this.

"So," she replied, "are you saying that you would like to see where we can take this, or am I misreading you entirely?"

He grinned. "I'm really bad at this, aren't I?" he asked in a conversational tone.

"Well, let's just say that I'm getting very, very confused—and very worried," Quinton replied.

"Worried?" he murmured, staring at her. "Why on earth worried?"

She shook her head. "Just in case it's not quite what I think it is."

He frowned and stared at her for a long moment, then picked up his glass of wine and said, "Well, I guess I'm just looking for a reassurance that you're prepared to go the distance, so that we can figure out exactly what we have."

"Absolutely," she replied immediately. "That's what I was hoping we were doing together."

"*Whew*," he said. "I'm glad to hear that because some days I haven't been too sure where you were at."

"And that's my fault. It was also brought home to me—again by my brother—that I haven't exactly explained what it was that I was looking for."

"Nope, you sure haven't." He smiled and gave a little shrug. "I didn't even want to push you now, but you could be leaving soon, as you told me not very long ago," he explained, "and things kind of hit me the wrong way that I might be once again in danger of losing you a second time."

"I wasn't planning on going too far," she said gently. "Only back into town."

"Only back into town, yes, and the occasional visit isn't quite what I was thinking of."

She frowned. "Well, if we're going out, presumably we would see each other a couple times a week?" she asked hopefully.

"Yeah, a couple times a week might be nice. Only I want more."

"You're the one who has this absolutely gorgeous place to live," she noted, her hand waving around at the complex. "We could meet here half the time and have dates in town too."

He grinned. "It is nice here, isn't it?"

"It's beautiful," she said. "It's a huge perk for you."

"It certainly made life a lot easier on me, as I've gotten the business going," he admitted. "It's also, in some ways, been a detriment because I'm always here, not in town, so it's hard to meet people."

"That's a good thing for me," she added, with feeling, "because that means you're still here."

He laughed. "Exactly. I'm still here, and I find that I'm still waiting."

"And what is it you're waiting for?"

He took a deep breath, reached across, laced her fingers with his, and said, "I don't know how you feel about this, but I feel like I've wasted enough time in my life hesitating, and I don't really want to hesitate anymore. So, for me, right now, I have a burning question that I don't want to wait any longer for an answer." He took a deep breath, and it just rushed out. "Would you marry me?"

She stared at him in shock, tears coming to the corners of her eyes. "Oh my God, are you serious?"

His gaze was locked on her face. "Of course I'm serious. It's hardly something to joke about."

Her jaw worked, almost as if she didn't know what to say.

And he felt the pain inside him clenching down tighter and tighter. "Oh, God." He starting to pull his hand away. "You really don't care like I care, do you?"

Then she grabbed his hand, pulled it up to her lips, and kissed it. "I didn't think you'd ever say it," she whispered. "Eight years ago I didn't think you'd ever say it."

"Eight years ago we weren't ready for that," he said. "You were just out of the denial stage about your accident and taking baby steps toward healing. And me? I had taken on this clinic by myself. I was overwhelmed, but Dani stood by both of us."

She thought back, smiled, and nodded her head. "You're right. We weren't on steady ground yet in our own lives, were we?" she asked. "We were still working on our own careers. I wanted to heal so I could light the world on fire as a lawyer and take on so many things and do so much," she shared. "And I got bogged down in work and bogged down in life, and I came back to visit during that time, but there was always this distance between us," she murmured.

After a moment of complete silence, Stan mentioned, "You haven't answered me. ... And, dear God, that lack of an answer is making my stomach churn in all kinds of ways that I don't like."

She looked up at him, tears in her eyes. As one slowly dripped down her cheek, she nodded and whispered, "Please."

He looked at her and asked, "Is that a yes?"

"It's a yes."

He shouted it louder. "Is that a yes?"

"It's a yes!" she shouted.

And he did it one more time at the top of his lungs, and, when she shouted right back, "It was a yes!" the entire place burst into cheers.

Startled, the two of them turned and looked around to see everybody leaning over the railing up on the deck area, staring down at them at the pool, clapping their hearts out.

Quinton clasped her hands over her mouth and whispered, "Oh, my God, they heard us."

Stan laughed and laughed. "We were shouting it from the top of our lungs," he noted in complete joy.

She grinned. "We were, weren't we?"

He got up, walked around, threw his arms around her, and gave her a warm hug.

She sat, just nestled in his arms, the tears running down her face, wondering how life had suddenly become so perfect.

"You're perfect, you know that, right?" he murmured. She went to shake her head, and he immediately placed his hands on either side of her head to clasp it so that she couldn't. "Just respond with, *Yes, Stan, I realize that.*"

She burst out laughing. "Let me just say, I'm working on

it."

"And that's fine," he said. "At least that's the truth."

"And you won't let me have it any other way, will you?" she asked, chuckling.

"Absolutely not," he stated, "because, for me, you've been perfect right since the first day you arrived. I just didn't know how to get there."

"Well, guess what? You didn't do half bad at all. You got there."

He leaned down, gave her a big kiss, and added, "And, if you're *reeaally* nice, we might get you to move in here—at least for a few years once we're married, while we figure out what we want to do after this."

She stared at him, looked around at Hathaway House, and chuckled. "You'd better watch it," she teased. "You know that some people might say I married you just for that."

He laughed and laughed, held her close to his heart, and added, "You know something? That's fine. It just gives me a longer time to win you over into my heart."

She patted his chest. "No winning needed. Honestly, I've been trying to get there since forever."

He clasped her hand tighter against his chest and whispered, "News flash, you've been there since forever. You just didn't know it." As the cheers up above died down, he looked up and yelled, "You're all invited." At that, the cheers started again.

She laughed and gasped. "Oh my gosh, a wedding."

"Yep, a wedding," he agreed. "I know there'll be a whole mess of them happening around here soon," he noted.

"I'd like my brother to be a little bit better first."

"Your brother will be your brother, and either he'll make

it or he won't," Stan stated, "but, given what I've seen lately, I have every confidence that he's a changed man."

"You know what? I think you're right," she agreed gently. "And that fills my heart with joy too."

"Besides, I'm sure he'll be more than happy to attend his sister's wedding."

"I think so too," she said.

"I know so," Stan replied firmly. "When the chips are down, it's still family that counts. And, in all ways, he's your brother."

She smiled, curled up in Stan's arms, and he thought life had never been better. As music came from above, somebody playing the Wedding March, Stan looked up to see Dennis walking down the stairs with a bottle of champagne, two flutes, and some fancy creation on a plate. Stan nudged Quinton. "Take a look at that."

"Oh my gosh," she said in awe, when Dennis reached them. "That is stunning," she said in a tone of absolute mystified confusion. "Did you just whip that up?"

"Yeah, we have so many loving scenarios happening here now that we must keep them on tap." She stared at him uncomprehendingly, and he burst out laughing. "I'm just kidding. No, I put this up for the two of you. It's a great night, and you both need some champagne to celebrate this special moment."

She looked up, smiled, and said, "Thank you."

He shook his head. "No, thank you. Whenever somebody finds their way home," he said, "it's a lesson for all of us to keep the light on because we never really know who needs it." And, with those words of wisdom, he leaned over, gave her a hug, and raced back up to the dining room, leaving the two of them alone to enjoy a few moments as they started the rest of their life. Together.

Epilogue

RYATT STARED AT his sister. "Seriously? You're getting married?"

More change and mixed feelings slammed into him. But she deserved this, and he was so happy for her. "I'm really delighted," he said. "Yeah, it kind of shook me there for a moment. You know how I feel about change and all, but this is a good change. The family needs to grow, and this is something that I think would be really good for you. He obviously adores you."

She laughed. "I don't know how that came to be, but, yes, I think you're right."

"No thinking about it. That man is unbelievably hooked."

She smiled. "Well, it's nice to know," she murmured. "He's a very special man."

"And I agree. Absolutely I would love to be part of your wedding," he told her. "Don't make it too soon, and I might even manage to walk down the aisle."

"I'm not making it too soon," she agreed, "because you can bet I'm going to walk down it too."

He laughed at that. "Well, now we have goals," he stated. "I'm seriously delighted for you."

And, when she took off, a beaming smile took over his face. He sank down onto the bed, stunned at the turn of events. He didn't even know why he was so shocked. It was obvious that the two of them were meant for each other; maybe it was just the speed of it that shook him. And, of course, he'd just said goodbye to somebody in his life— somebody he really had no business even hanging on to— and here his sister was now making more change happening.

Ryatt wasn't very good with change; he knew that. He was working on it, but he wasn't there yet. However, he would get there. He definitely would get there. When a knock came on his doorframe, he looked up to see a small redhead, her single braid hanging down the front of her shirt. He smiled and asked, "Hi, what can I do for you?"

"Well, if you're up for it, I have paperwork for you to sign."

That was not what he wanted. He glared at her. "Great way to ruin the day."

She shrugged. "Yet it needs to be done. And I promise, afterward I'll get out of your hair."

Pinching the bridge of his nose, he tried to convince himself that it wasn't her fault that his joy over his sister's upcoming nuptials were now a distant memory, and that reality was hitting him with a bite. "What is the paperwork for?"

"You asked for a transfer, I believe." Her tone was innocent, but a wary look filled her gaze. She set the paperwork on the small table at his side. "I'll leave these with you. When you're done, you can contact anyone in the office or bring them down yourself." And she quickly backed up to the door.

"I'm not transferring," he snapped, and his tone brooked no argument. "Yeah, I was pissed. Yeah, I was in an ugly mood, but I wasn't serious."

She stared at him, nodded, and whispered, "Got it. I'll let Dani know." And, with that, she disappeared.

Ryatt swore at his unruly bad temper, his lack of patience, and the situation that had stretched his new sense of calm to morph him into an angry bear.

Dani had actually called his bluff.

Good for her but not for him. He'd have to fix this.

And fast.

This concludes Book 17 of Hathaway House: Quinton.
Read about Ryatt: Hathaway House, Book 18

Hathaway House: Ryatt (Book #18)

Welcome to Hathaway House. Rehab Center. Safe Haven. Second chance at life and love.

After a rough start at Hathaway House and a major reboot in attitude, Ryatt still struggles to get his feet under him at the center. Seeing his sister back here hit him harder than he expected. He would like to think that, once here, he had a free pass for the rest of his life—but apparently not. Now he needs to see real progress, everlasting change, to make that future for himself that he's rather desperate to have.

Lana always looked at life with a happy, fun-loving attitude. She loves working at Hathaway and interacting with the patients and staff. It's heartwarming and rewarding work. Every once in a while she finds a patient who is reticent and even grumpy. That fits Ryatt, but she's attracted to the dark broken depths of him.

But can she show him another way to live and to view the world? She hopes so, as he's already helped her to see so much more in her own.

Find Book 18 here!

To find out more visit Dale Mayer's website.

https://geni.us/DMRyattUniversal

Author's Note

Thank you for reading Quinton: Hathaway House, Book 17! If you enjoyed the book, please take a moment and leave a short review.

Dear reader,

I love to hear from readers, and you can contact me at my website: www.dalemayer.com or at my Facebook author page. To be informed of new releases and special offers, sign up for my newsletter or follow me on BookBub. And if you are interested in joining Dale Mayer's Reader Group, here is the Facebook sign up page.
http://geni.us/DaleMayerFBGroup

Cheers,
Dale Mayer

About the Author

Dale Mayer is a *USA Today* best-selling author, best known for her SEALs military romances, her Psychic Visions series, and her Lovely Lethal Garden cozy series. Her contemporary romances are raw and full of passion and emotion (Broken But … Mending, Hathaway House series). Her thrillers will keep you guessing (Kate Morgan, By Death series), and her romantic comedies will keep you giggling (*It's a Dog's Life*, a stand-alone novella; and the Broken Protocols series, starring Charming Marvin, the cat).

Dale honors the stories that come to her—and some of them are crazy, break all the rules and cross multiple genres!

To go with her fiction, she also writes nonfiction in many different fields, with books available on résumé writing, companion gardening, and the US mortgage system. All her books are available in print and ebook format.

Connect with Dale Mayer Online

Dale's Website – www.dalemayer.com

Twitter – @DaleMayer

Facebook Page – geni.us/DaleMayerFBFanPage

Facebook Group – geni.us/DaleMayerFBGroup

BookBub – geni.us/DaleMayerBookbub

Instagram – geni.us/DaleMayerInstagram

Goodreads – geni.us/DaleMayerGoodreads

Newsletter – geni.us/DaleNews

Also by Dale Mayer

Published Adult Books:

Shadow Recon
Magnus, Book 1

Bullard's Battle
Ryland's Reach, Book 1
Cain's Cross, Book 2
Eton's Escape, Book 3
Garret's Gambit, Book 4
Kano's Keep, Book 5
Fallon's Flaw, Book 6
Quinn's Quest, Book 7
Bullard's Beauty, Book 8
Bullard's Best, Book 9
Bullard's Battle, Books 1–2
Bullard's Battle, Books 3–4
Bullard's Battle, Books 5–6
Bullard's Battle, Books 7–8

Terkel's Team
Damon's Deal, Book 1
Wade's War, Book 2
Gage's Goal, Book 3
Calum's Contact, Book 4
Rick's Road, Book 5
Scott's Summit, Book 6

Kate Morgan

Simon Says… Hide, Book 1
Simon Says… Jump, Book 2
Simon Says… Ride, Book 3
Simon Says… Scream, Book 4
Simon Says… Run, Book 5

Hathaway House

Aaron, Book 1
Brock, Book 2
Cole, Book 3
Denton, Book 4
Elliot, Book 5
Finn, Book 6
Gregory, Book 7
Heath, Book 8
Iain, Book 9
Jaden, Book 10
Keith, Book 11
Lance, Book 12
Melissa, Book 13
Nash, Book 14
Owen, Book 15
Percy, Book 16
Quinton, Book 17
Ryatt, Book 18
Hathaway House, Books 1–3
Hathaway House, Books 4–6
Hathaway House, Books 7–9

The K9 Files

Ethan, Book 1
Pierce, Book 2

Zane, Book 3

Blaze, Book 4

Lucas, Book 5

Parker, Book 6

Carter, Book 7

Weston, Book 8

Greyson, Book 9

Rowan, Book 10

Caleb, Book 11

Kurt, Book 12

Tucker, Book 13

Harley, Book 14

Kyron, Book 15

Jenner, Book 16

Rhys, Book 17

The K9 Files, Books 1–2

The K9 Files, Books 3–4

The K9 Files, Books 5–6

The K9 Files, Books 7–8

The K9 Files, Books 9–10

The K9 Files, Books 11–12

Lovely Lethal Gardens

Arsenic in the Azaleas, Book 1

Bones in the Begonias, Book 2

Corpse in the Carnations, Book 3

Daggers in the Dahlias, Book 4

Evidence in the Echinacea, Book 5

Footprints in the Ferns, Book 6

Gun in the Gardenias, Book 7

Handcuffs in the Heather, Book 8

Ice Pick in the Ivy, Book 9

Jewels in the Juniper, Book 10
Killer in the Kiwis, Book 11
Lifeless in the Lilies, Book 12
Murder in the Marigolds, Book 13
Nabbed in the Nasturtiums, Book 14
Offed in the Orchids, Book 15
Poison in the Pansies, Book 16
Quarry in the Quince, Book 17
Revenge in the Roses, Book 18
Lovely Lethal Gardens, Books 1–2
Lovely Lethal Gardens, Books 3–4
Lovely Lethal Gardens, Books 5–6
Lovely Lethal Gardens, Books 7–8
Lovely Lethal Gardens, Books 9–10

Psychic Vision Series
Tuesday's Child
Hide 'n Go Seek
Maddy's Floor
Garden of Sorrow
Knock Knock…
Rare Find
Eyes to the Soul
Now You See Her
Shattered
Into the Abyss
Seeds of Malice
Eye of the Falcon
Itsy-Bitsy Spider
Unmasked
Deep Beneath
From the Ashes

Stroke of Death
Ice Maiden
Snap, Crackle…
What If…
Talking Bones
String of Tears
Psychic Visions Books 1–3
Psychic Visions Books 4–6
Psychic Visions Books 7–9

By Death Series
Touched by Death
Haunted by Death
Chilled by Death
By Death Books 1–3

Broken Protocols – Romantic Comedy Series
Cat's Meow
Cat's Pajamas
Cat's Cradle
Cat's Claus
Broken Protocols 1-4

Broken and… Mending
Skin
Scars
Scales (of Justice)
Broken but… Mending 1-3

Glory
Genesis
Tori
Celeste

Glory Trilogy

Biker Blues

Morgan: Biker Blues, Volume 1
Cash: Biker Blues, Volume 2

SEALs of Honor

Mason: SEALs of Honor, Book 1
Hawk: SEALs of Honor, Book 2
Dane: SEALs of Honor, Book 3
Swede: SEALs of Honor, Book 4
Shadow: SEALs of Honor, Book 5
Cooper: SEALs of Honor, Book 6
Markus: SEALs of Honor, Book 7
Evan: SEALs of Honor, Book 8
Mason's Wish: SEALs of Honor, Book 9
Chase: SEALs of Honor, Book 10
Brett: SEALs of Honor, Book 11
Devlin: SEALs of Honor, Book 12
Easton: SEALs of Honor, Book 13
Ryder: SEALs of Honor, Book 14
Macklin: SEALs of Honor, Book 15
Corey: SEALs of Honor, Book 16
Warrick: SEALs of Honor, Book 17
Tanner: SEALs of Honor, Book 18
Jackson: SEALs of Honor, Book 19
Kanen: SEALs of Honor, Book 20
Nelson: SEALs of Honor, Book 21
Taylor: SEALs of Honor, Book 22
Colton: SEALs of Honor, Book 23
Troy: SEALs of Honor, Book 24
Axel: SEALs of Honor, Book 25
Baylor: SEALs of Honor, Book 26

Hudson: SEALs of Honor, Book 27

Lachlan: SEALs of Honor, Book 28

Paxton: SEALs of Honor, Book 29

SEALs of Honor, Books 1–3

SEALs of Honor, Books 4–6

SEALs of Honor, Books 7–10

SEALs of Honor, Books 11–13

SEALs of Honor, Books 14–16

SEALs of Honor, Books 17–19

SEALs of Honor, Books 20–22

SEALs of Honor, Books 23–25

Heroes for Hire

Levi's Legend: Heroes for Hire, Book 1

Stone's Surrender: Heroes for Hire, Book 2

Merk's Mistake: Heroes for Hire, Book 3

Rhodes's Reward: Heroes for Hire, Book 4

Flynn's Firecracker: Heroes for Hire, Book 5

Logan's Light: Heroes for Hire, Book 6

Harrison's Heart: Heroes for Hire, Book 7

Saul's Sweetheart: Heroes for Hire, Book 8

Dakota's Delight: Heroes for Hire, Book 9

Tyson's Treasure: Heroes for Hire, Book 10

Jace's Jewel: Heroes for Hire, Book 11

Rory's Rose: Heroes for Hire, Book 12

Brandon's Bliss: Heroes for Hire, Book 13

Liam's Lily: Heroes for Hire, Book 14

North's Nikki: Heroes for Hire, Book 15

Anders's Angel: Heroes for Hire, Book 16

Reyes's Raina: Heroes for Hire, Book 17

Dezi's Diamond: Heroes for Hire, Book 18

Vince's Vixen: Heroes for Hire, Book 19

Ice's Icing: Heroes for Hire, Book 20
Johan's Joy: Heroes for Hire, Book 21
Galen's Gemma: Heroes for Hire, Book 22
Zack's Zest: Heroes for Hire, Book 23
Bonaparte's Belle: Heroes for Hire, Book 24
Noah's Nemesis: Heroes for Hire, Book 25
Tomas's Trials: Heroes for Hire, Book 26
Carson's Choice: Heroes for Hire, Book 27
Dante's Decision: Heroes for Hire, Book 28
Heroes for Hire, Books 1–3
Heroes for Hire, Books 4–6
Heroes for Hire, Books 7–9
Heroes for Hire, Books 10–12
Heroes for Hire, Books 13–15
Heroes for Hire, Books 16–18
Heroes for Hire, Books 19–21
Heroes for Hire, Books 22–24

SEALs of Steel
Badger: SEALs of Steel, Book 1
Erick: SEALs of Steel, Book 2
Cade: SEALs of Steel, Book 3
Talon: SEALs of Steel, Book 4
Laszlo: SEALs of Steel, Book 5
Geir: SEALs of Steel, Book 6
Jager: SEALs of Steel, Book 7
The Final Reveal: SEALs of Steel, Book 8
SEALs of Steel, Books 1–4
SEALs of Steel, Books 5–8
SEALs of Steel, Books 1–8

The Mavericks
Kerrick, Book 1

Griffin, Book 2

Jax, Book 3

Beau, Book 4

Asher, Book 5

Ryker, Book 6

Miles, Book 7

Nico, Book 8

Keane, Book 9

Lennox, Book 10

Gavin, Book 11

Shane, Book 12

Diesel, Book 13

Jerricho, Book 14

Killian, Book 15

Hatch, Book 16

Corbin, Book 17

Aiden, Book 18

The Mavericks, Books 1–2

The Mavericks, Books 3–4

The Mavericks, Books 5–6

The Mavericks, Books 7–8

The Mavericks, Books 9–10

The Mavericks, Books 11–12

Collections

Dare to Be You…

Dare to Love…

Dare to be Strong…

RomanceX3

Standalone Novellas

It's a Dog's Life

Riana's Revenge

Second Chances

Published Young Adult Books:

Family Blood Ties Series
Vampire in Denial
Vampire in Distress
Vampire in Design
Vampire in Deceit
Vampire in Defiance
Vampire in Conflict
Vampire in Chaos
Vampire in Crisis
Vampire in Control
Vampire in Charge
Family Blood Ties Set 1–3
Family Blood Ties Set 1–5
Family Blood Ties Set 4–6
Family Blood Ties Set 7–9
Sian's Solution, A Family Blood Ties Series Prequel
    Novelette

Design series
Dangerous Designs
Deadly Designs
Darkest Designs
Design Series Trilogy

Standalone
In Cassie's Corner
Gem Stone (a Gemma Stone Mystery)
Time Thieves

Published Non-Fiction Books:

Career Essentials

Career Essentials: The Résumé
Career Essentials: The Cover Letter
Career Essentials: The Interview
Career Essentials: 3 in 1